Distracted

Alexandra Warren

Distracted

Acknowledgements

Thanking God first, knowing none of this would be possible without his blessing.

I made it to book baby #8! And this is probably my favorite one, even though I usually feel that way after every release. Lol

But this one I hold near and dear because it was the first time that a character was like, "Yo… tell my story. I got somethin' for you right now if you want it."
And boy, did Bryson give me a run for my money!

So I hope you all enjoy reading it as much I enjoyed writing it.

Bryson

"Damn, that was good."

I looked over to Madeline who was sprawled out across the bed, stuck in the exact position I had left her in after hitting it from the back. I felt bad for the girl, knowing I was going to have to fire her now that we had crossed a line we could never recover from.

But... it wasn't the first time.

"I can't believe you made me wait that long for a taste of B-Money," she replied between breaths, still exhausted from our impromptu session. It was something like a badge of honor to hear her satisfaction, but I knew the bliss would be short-lived once I broke the news.

"Considering you needed the paychecks, you better be glad I made you wait that long."

She sat up, pulling the cover over her naked body before asking, "What's that supposed to mean?"

"Well, business and pleasure don't mix for me, so I gotta cut one. And for you, that'd be the business part." I honestly hated that I had let things get this far, especially since Madeline had only been my employee for a couple of weeks now.

"What? Are you kidding me, Bryson? I work my ass off to make sure you're dressed to the nines."

I was pretty sure I could pick out my own clothes. But since my do-it-all agent, Leslie, prided herself on keeping my image clean, we had decided to hire Madeline as my stylist; though it was pretty clear from the jump that she was more interested in *me* than my clothes.

"No offense, but uhh… it's really not that hard."

She smacked her teeth before she hopped out of my bed and snatched her clothes off the ground. Since I didn't want to put bad energy out there in the world, I gave her a sincere, "I'm sorry, Maddy."

She rolled her pond blue eyes, adjusting her clothes in my floor-length mirror as she said, "Whatever. Just make sure the check comes on time. Some of us have bills to pay."

I smiled as I assured her, "I'll even add in a little bonus for your exceptional tongue skills."

I thought of it as a compliment - a token of my appreciation - but it only seemed to piss her off even more as she spit out, "Fuck you, Bryson."

I climbed out of bed, grabbing my pajama pants and sliding them on before following her out of the room.

"Maddy, you didn't really think we were gonna work together and sleep together, did you?"

She didn't stop her trek to the door as she replied, "Obviously. Otherwise I wouldn't have fucked you."

"I'm pretty sure *I* fucked *you*, but that's beside the point."

Damn, there's that look again.

"Look, I don't mean to hurt your little feelings or nothin' like that, but we can't do this shit. And ain't no turnin' back after you fuck with somebody like me, so I gotta let you go." I didn't mean to sound cocky, but I had already learned its truth on so many occasions.

Too many occasions.

"Don't worry about letting me go. I quit."

"But… *you know what*? That actually works too. Send me your letter of resignation and shit. I know my peoples will ask for it." I could already see Leslie now,

—

2

rolling her eyes when she received the letter on her desk. "You're probably fuckin' her too!"

There was no way in hell I would even think about touching Leslie, especially considering she was happily married to a woman. But instead of giving her that tidbit of information, I simply told her, "Nah. She has a way of keeping me in my place by not being easy."

Madeline stopped right in the doorframe to scowl at me. "Did I already tell you to go fuck yourself?"

I shrugged. "Well... I would do that. But I already fucked you so..."

She huffed and puffed, totally outdone by my truth. "Goodbye, Bryson!"

I watched her storm to her car as I replied, "Take care, Madeline." Which I really said more to myself than her since she was so far away.

In no time at all, her tires were screeching against the pavement of my driveway, and all I could do was shake my head.

Note to self: Add consensual sex clause to all female employee contracts.

—

3

Kennedy

"Damn, that was good."

I rolled over on my back, grinning from ear-to-ear as I thought about what had just happened for the third time tonight. Landon was an incredible lover - *had always been an incredible lover* - but that wasn't enough to keep me from wondering if our engagement was a mistake.

Welp, there goes my endorphin high...

Of course I loved him, and he loved me back. But in the back of my head, I knew something was missing.

That spark, the butterflies, the fullness of my heart.

It seemed as if it had all gone away the day after he proposed. I initially assumed it had something to do with the general nerves of planning a wedding. But as more time passed, I began to wonder if maybe I just wasn't ready to take that next step.

I mean, me... a wife?

Changing my last name?

Sharing accounts and picking out houses?

All of it sounded so... *far-fetched.*

But I couldn't let Landon know that.

He was patiently waiting for the day to make me Mrs. Landon Montgomery, make me a mommy, make me his for life.

Damn, that's scary.

I looked over to him just as he turned onto his side and began to snore. Giving a smirk of satisfaction, I tiptoed out of bed, stopping by the bathroom to clean myself up before putting on my robe and heading to the living room. I thought about stopping by the kitchen to make myself a sandwich, but I was quickly reminded of the wedding dress that I had been avoiding trying on knowing my body wasn't ready for it.

Hell, *I* wasn't ready for it, so of course my body didn't want to comply.

But... I'd have to get over it.

This was happening.

It was real.

I turned on the TV, flipping through channel after channel of nothingness until I ended up on Landon's favorite channel, *ESPN.* You'd think he'd be tired of the re-runs of *SportsCenter*, but that didn't stop him from watching it every time it came on.

Naturally, I had grown fond of it as well.

Well, enough to watch at least one run-through of it.

It was *NBA* season, and while most people were excited to see the stats and highlights, I was excited to see what everyone was wearing when they showed up to the arena. Being a personal stylist was my calling long before I knew it was a profession that people actually made money from. I was the friend people called when they had to be on point for an event, or when they wanted to land a new gig and needed to dress to impress, *or* when they were trying to get their back blown out without dressing like a complete slut. I was the one who studied designers and actually cared about the names people were wearing on the red carpet. I had so many subscriptions to different fashion magazines that I'd often catch onto trends late because my piles were so backed up.

I was sure doing the job professionally would be a piece of cake if I just tried it. But who would pick a stylist with no formal experience other than my job in retail, no relevant degree, and no fashion-related references?

—

Nobody, that's who.

Not that I had applied for any positions to find out if that was actually true. But in my head, I had already visualized the polite ass rejection letters.

Sorry. You can dress your ass off, but we can't trust you.

Thanks for applying, but we've already hired someone who's way better than you.

We appreciate your interest, but you'd be a fool to think we'd let you have the job with that shitty ass resume.

I snagged my laptop off the coffee table and turned it on, knowing it wouldn't hurt to at least take a peek at what jobs were out there.

As I waited for it to load, my eyes flashed back to the TV screen. They were interviewing some guy named Bryson Harris according to the subtitle on the side of the screen, but I was more focused on his outfit. The color scheme of his plum sports jacket and light blue dress shirt complemented his skin tone well, but I wasn't quite feelin' the fitted pants and tennis shoes combination. I knew if he was my client, I would've probably picked loafers.

Or, at least a clean dress shoe.

I could so do that.

Now that my computer was ready for action, I went straight to *Google* and typed in *Stylist Jobs in Philadelphia*. A bunch of typical stuff came up - stuff I should've been aiming for considering I technically had no experience in the industry - but that wasn't what I wanted.

I wanted to do it big.

I scrolled through the most recent listings until I found exactly what I was looking for. And after allowing my finger to hover over my mouse for a solid three

—

minutes straight, I used dick-courage to submit my
resume.

Bryson

"Will you please do me a favor and stop thinking with your damn dick? You know good and well that girl doesn't deserve the job, not to mention she'd probably be fired faster than that last hooch you insisted on hiring."

I knew my right-hand woman was right, though I couldn't blow up her ego by giving her all the credit.

"Leslie, you helped me hire her. Said she'd be good for the image. And you thought she was pretty too, so quit trippin'."

She rolled her eyes at me as usual before going to get the next interviewee from the lobby. I wasn't sure why I even needed to be there since Leslie didn't usually trust my opinion anyway. But here I was, spending my only off-day of the week interviewing a bunch of women vying for the job as my personal stylist.

While I waited for her to return, I made myself busy on *Instagram*, scrolling through the Explore page for a girl to take to a movie premiere I had been invited to out in LA. I thought about calling my friend Alexis, but there was hardly any chance she'd actually go for it considering we had technically fallen out.

"*Ahem...* Bryson?"

I hadn't even noticed anyone come in.

I scrolled a few final swipes on my phone before I answered, "Yeah?"

"Bryson, this is Kennedy."

I stood up to be polite, but more importantly to get a better look at the girl.

She was… *cute.*

Her body was as lanky as they came, and she had the most innocent face that I could hardly see her doing wrong if she tried. Her hair was pulled back into a ponytail, putting her high cheekbones on display; cheekbones that created a direct path to her luscious lips that were colored a bright shade of red.

Probably one of those Rihanna colors.

I rounded the table and stuck my hand out to her as I introduced myself, "Bryson Harris. Pleasure to meet you, Kennedy."

Her eyes were almost as bright as the smile she gave when she returned my handshake, her small hand disappearing in my massive one. "And you as well, Mr. Harris."

Mr. Harris, huh?

I could get used to that shit.

Leslie must've seen the wheels turning in my head as she quickly intervened, "Kennedy, you can have a seat here. Would you like a bottle of water or anything before we get started?"

"Please," she piped out in a voice right above a whisper as if she was suddenly nervous.

"No problem. I'll be right back."

Leslie made it to the doorway, but not without turning around to issue me a warning glare. I wasn't sure why she thought I'd be on anything other than my best behavior.

Actually, I take that back.

Leslie wasn't blind.

She could clearly see how attractive Kennedy was, so of course she wanted to warn me about spittin' game to the girl before we could even figure out if she was any good.

Speaking of which…

—

10

"So Kennedy, how long have you been a stylist?" I asked as I returned to my seat on the other side of the table.

"*Informally*? For as long as I can remember."

"What about formally?"

"Umm... well, this is actually the first time I've interviewed for a personal stylist position, so I don't *technically* have any experience."

I could see a hint of sadness on her face as if she was assuming that lone fact was going to take her out of the competition.

"I see. So have you ever styled anyone of my caliber? You know... freelancing or anything like that?"

She shook her head. "No. You'd be the first one I could get my hands on. *I mean*... not like that. I'm sorry, did I offend you?"

I couldn't help but smile at her apology. It certainly took a lot more than something like that to offend me. And to be real, there was *nothing* offensive about the concept of her putting her hands on me.

So I licked my lips as I confidently answered, "Not at all, Kennedy."

She blushed instantly, casting her eyes down to her lap and sweeping a stray hair behind her ear.

Before I could dig any deeper, Leslie returned with the water.

"So Kennedy, how many..."

"She's hired."

"What?" The two women spoke simultaneously.

"I said she's hired. I want her to be my stylist."

Kennedy could hardly contain herself, looking like a kid who had just been invited to *Disney World* as she replied, "Are you serious?! I mean, *wow*."

Leslie's eyes burned into me as if I was making the most reckless decision she had ever heard of. "But we

—

11

haven't even done the interview yet, Bryson."

I knew it was probably a little crazy of me to hire the girl without knowing anything about her. But the fact that she was new and untapped as far as the fashion world was concerned had me intrigued.

Well, that along with how cute she was.

"I know all I need to know. She's an up-and-comer. Someone who hasn't been given the opportunity to put her mark on the industry yet. I'll be her guinea pig."

My eyes flashed over to Kennedy who looked flattered by my words. And even though that wasn't my intention, it definitely made me feel good to see her so happy.

Still, that wasn't enough to stop Leslie's scolding. "Bryson, we are working really hard to…"

I cut her off. "Leslie, she's our girl." Then I turned to Kennedy and asked, "Do you accept the offer? We can negotiate PTO, and benefits, and all that other boring stuff later. But will you… be my *personal* stylist?"

She looked me directly in my eyes, giving me weird little tingles as she answered with the proudest smile, "I'd love to."

Kennedy

"Congratulations, babe!"

Landon pulled me into a big hug the second I walked into our apartment. I had called him on my way home from the interview, desperate to share the news of my new position with somebody. It was almost unbelievable that they had decided to take a chance on me, but I was more than grateful for the opportunity.

"Thank you. Thank you very much," I replied, serving my best Elvis impression.

"So what's next? Do you get season tickets? Tell me all about it."

I really wasn't ready to talk about *that* part of the job for two reasons. For one, I really didn't have the answers yet. And for two, I hated that Bryson was still on my mind for reasons other than the job. I wasn't even nervous going into the interview; more optimistic than anything. But the second I saw him, with his long, muscular, tattooed frame just waiting for me to tend to his... *needs.*

His fashion needs, that is.

I swallowed hard to wash away those thoughts before I answered, "I'm not sure yet, Landon. They're gonna send me all the employee info via email some time tomorrow."

"So did you get to meet him?!"

I knew exactly who he was talking about, but I played dumb. "Meet who?"

"Bryson Harris. That's who the job is for, right? You

know he's one of my favorite players."

Landon's list of supposed favorite players changed so often I could hardly keep up.

"Oh yeah. Yeah, he was there. He umm... he hired me on the spot." I said it in a low tone on purpose, hoping he wouldn't catch it.

But he did.

"You're shittin' me! That's great, babe! I'm so proud of you, future wifey."

My stomach turned at that one.

I mean, what kind of future wife was I thinking about another man who I knew nothing about other than the fact that I'd get to dress him up like my own personal Ken doll?

Instead of basking in my guilt, I changed the subject. "How about we go out for a drink to celebrate?"

Landon's face changed from excited to gloomy as he replied, "I wish I could, babe. But I picked up a shift tonight at the club."

The club was short for the upscale gentlemen's club his uncle, Lionel, owned. Even though Landon had a regular day job as a high school math teacher, he still picked up shifts from time to time to bring in some extra money. It wasn't the worst place in the world, especially since the dancers weren't completely nude and he only had to sweep up money all night. But I still wasn't thrilled about the idea of spending one of the most exciting nights of my life alone.

So I brushed it off, wrapping my arms around his neck as I told him, "He's family, Landon. I'm sure he'll understand if you cancel."

He looked down at me with a smile, wrapping his arms around my waist before giving me a quick kiss. I thought he was convinced until he replied, "Well I would, but I really need the money since we decided to, you know… get married." *My damn stomach.* "Wedding isn't gonna pay for itself, right?"

He had a point, though I hated to admit it. My parents were hardworking people, but they certainly couldn't afford the wedding I had in mind. "Well hopefully with the extra money I'll be bringing in, you'll be able to quit the club for good."

He wore a halfhearted smile as he said, "Yeah, I hope so too, babe. But don't let me stop your shine. Why don't you call some of your friends and go out on the town?"

My face turned stank on its own.

"*Friends?* What are those?"

I could hardly call any of the ladies I hung out with friends. They were more like associates; always down to go out and have a good time, but not really about anything substantial. Like… none of them were qualified to be the Godmother of my future children.

But my personal opinion wasn't enough to stop Landon from groaning, "Kennedy…"

"Fine. I'll go out. You be safe at the club. And tell Uncle Lionel I said hello."

Never again.

I should've known it wasn't a good idea to bring my girl Chloe out fresh off of her break-up, but she was my last resort after my first two options flew out of the window thanks to the lack of a babysitter and being in between hair appointments.

"He's such a piece of shit, Kenn! I mean, he knew I saw the girl climb out of the window and he still had the nerve to claim I was seeing shit. But I saw her ass, Kenn. I know I did."

I took the longest sip of my cocktail as I tried to come up with some surely terrible reply. Part of the reason I couldn't stand hanging out with the girls was because all they wanted to talk about was man drama. You'd hardly believe these girls were *ever* happy in their relationships with the way they acted; though with Chloe's situation, her unhappiness actually made sense.

"Maybe it was a burglar," I tossed out before closing my lips over my straw.

"What?!"

This time, I gave her the complete version. "Maybe it was a burglar you saw climbing out of the window."

Chloe looked ready to slap me as she said, "Kennedy, you can *not* be serious right now. *A burglar?* You almost sound as bad as him!"

See what I mean?

Terrible.

I didn't understand drama well enough to be able to contribute to the solution, especially when no one really wanted to hear a solution. They just wanted someone to cheer on their speculation.

So instead of providing a rebuttal, I started something fresh. "Well, what are you gonna do about it?"

She took a sip of her Rum and Coke before she answered, "I'm gonna go over there, get my shit, and move into a hotel until he fesses up the truth."

It sounded all fine and dandy, but I knew how easily those type of plans usually flew out of the window. Especially with good, consistent dick on the line.

"And then what?"

"Then I'm gonna... I don't know, Kennedy. What should I do?"

I thought long and hard, providing the only answer that came to mind. "I'm... not the one you should be asking. In fact, I'm probably the last person you should

—

16

be asking."

She brushed me off. "Oh, that's right. You have the perfect future husband, with the perfect ass engagement ring, and the perfect happily ever after. You wouldn't know the struggle if it bopped you on the head."

My initial reaction was along the lines of *"fuck you, jealous bitch"*, but I held it in for the sake of the night. I was supposed to be celebrating, not engaging in an argument with the only "friend" I could get out of the house.

So instead I teased, "I'd probably recognize it then, but you know what? That's beside the point. If you need a place to stay or whatever, you know you always have a couch at my crib." I was really only offering it out of respect, not because I actually wanted her crazy ass staying in my apartment.

"Thanks, Kennedy. That's why you're my girl," she said, clanking her glass against mine.

I was just getting ready to put my straw to my lips for another long drag when I heard, "Kennedy?"

I turned around and had to tilt my head back to find his eyes.

Mistake #1.

Bryson's eyes were beautiful; so beautiful that I already knew what color handkerchiefs I wanted to use to complement his dressier ensembles.

Stop it, Kennedy!

"Mr. Harris! Hi!" I piped out nervously, standing to give him a handshake under Chloe's watchful eye. I certainly didn't want her to get the wrong impression.

"Kennedy, please. Bryson is more than fine," he replied, totally ignoring my extended hand as he pulled me in for a quick hug.

Damn, he even feels good.

"I'm... I'm sorry. Hi, Bryson. I like your outfit, but

17

we have to get this shoe situation under control. I mean, tennis shoes again? You're better than that."

I couldn't wait to have full reign over him.

I mean... *his wardrobe choices.*

"Damn, girl. You aren't on the clock tonight," he said with a laugh that rumbled all over my skin. I was embarrassed for more reasons than one, but mainly because of the way my body kept reacting to his every move.

I looked down at my own shoes as I pushed out, "Oh. Right. I'm sorry."

Again.

"And quit being so sorry. You're right. I didn't have to wear tennis shoes. But I guess that's what we'll be paying you for, right?" He completed his sentence with a swipe down my bare arm that gave me tingles instantly.

Mistake #2.

I tried to focus on something other than my burning skin as I pushed out, "Right."

"Hey, why don't you and your friend come up to VIP with us? The sound is better and the drinks are free."

Though I knew I probably should've stopped with the first Long Island, drinks on my boss's tab didn't sound like the worst idea in the world.

"We'll come!"

Wait what?

I looked over to Chloe who was already standing up, smoothing out her form-fitting dress with her eyes glued on the guy behind Bryson.

Bryson looked between the two with a goofy little smirk before directing his attention back to me.

"Cool. Let's roll then."

Bryson

"You can't possibly be this quiet all the time."

I figured Kennedy was pretty reserved, but her bangin' ass outfit completely contradicted that persona. The way her dress was fitting in all the right places gave me instant thoughts of being able to see what kind of body was hiding under it. But her energy... *that* read more like a shy, Catholic school girl.

They did used to say those girls were the biggest freaks, though...

I watched as she licked her lips nervously before she replied, "I'm sorry. I was just... listening to the music."

"And will you quit with all that sorry talk? Don't be sorry for doing what the hell you wanna do."

She nodded her head to confirm her understanding.

Instead of letting her go back into her silent groove, I asked, "You like this song?" I was familiar with the tune, but I didn't know the words nor who it was by.

She pulled a few strands of hair behind her ear as she answered, "Yeah. It's one of my favorites."

"Well if it's your favorite, shouldn't you be dancing to it?"

She rolled her eyes and her little hint of an attitude actually surprised me. "I don't dance, Bryson. I vibe, I groove, I chill, but I don't dance."

Yeah right.

I'd been around women enough to know that they all danced, or at least tried to dance. It just took the right person to bring it out of them.

"Kennedy, you dance. I know you do no matter how hard you're frontin' about it. So come on, let's dance."

I tried to pull her up off of the couch, but she remained glued as she said, "Bryson, I'm serious. I don't dance. I... *can't* dance."

"Well I'll teach you then. Now come on."

She sighed once she realized I wasn't giving up. I drug her out to the dance floor before flipping her around and pulling her long frame against mine. She followed my lead as I let my hands wrap around her waist and began grinding against her ass. She leaned further into me, adding more friction as we found our groove to the beat. And before I knew it, she was actually keeping up.

"I thought you said you couldn't dance?"

She visibly sighed, her shoulders dropping as she said, "I shouldn't be. *I'm...* I'm engaged."

I just know I didn't hear that right...

I looked down to her hand and didn't see a ring, so I figured I must've been trippin'.

And besides, she was here with me; *dancing* with me. So whatever she had going on must not have been much.

"Damn. You're incredible, Bryson."

Yeah, yeah, yeah, tell me somethin' new.

I couldn't believe I had ended up in bed with the girl, but I knew it didn't take much which meant I'd be cutting her off just as quickly as I had acquired her.

"You were good too, Hazel. Take your time gettin' up, love. I'll be back in a minute."

She blushed as she cuddled back into the sheets, more than likely getting ready to doze off. I'd let her get her rest for now. But in my head, I knew I'd be kicking her to the curb once the sun came up.

It was nothing personal. I just didn't want her to get the wrong idea that I was actually interested in a relationship with her. I mean, if she got with me on the first night, more than likely it wasn't her first time.

I left her in the room and headed to the kitchen to get some grub. I often kept music playing low throughout my house, but I could clearly hear that pesky little tune from the club. The song Kennedy loved enough to let her guard down and dance with me to.

Damn, she's so adorable.

I wasn't used to being attracted to the quiet types, so it honestly caught me off-guard. But I could tell there was a lot more to her than what she led on. She just needed somebody like me to bring it out of her.

I could hardly wait for the opportunity.

I grabbed a granola bar and a banana before I went to my home office and pulled up her contract. It was supposed to be the final draft, ready for sending first thing in the morning, but I knew I needed to add one more thing.

The one thing I forgot to include when I hired Madeline.

I had a strong feeling Kennedy would be tempting me to break my own rules sooner than later. The least I could do was make sure my ass was covered.

Kennedy

When I checked my email first thing in the morning, I just knew my eyes had to be playing tricks on me. I hadn't put my contacts in yet, so maybe my lack of complete 20/20 vision was causing an issue since there was no way I had read what I thought I read in the contract Bryson sent me from his personal email even though I was expecting it from Leslie.

I mean, he couldn't be serious, right?

Any consensual sex between Mr. Bryson Harris and Ms. Kennedy Wilson may be deemed grounds for immediate termination unless specified beforehand.

I read it a few times over to make sure I didn't miss the, *"Just kidding"*. But sure enough, that was nowhere to be found.

What kind of cocky son-of-a-bitch would even think about putting something like that in an employee contract?

Only someone like Bryson who could handpick his women - *employees included* - to meet his every need.

Considering he was a *NBA* champion, Rookie of the Year, *GQ* cover kind of guy, I really shouldn't have been surprised. I guess it was just the fact that my name was actually listed in print like I would even *think* about doing such a thing that bothered me.

Not that Bryson couldn't get it under other circumstances.

He definitely, *definitely* could.

That beard, those mystical eyes, the tattoos...

I bit my bottom lip a little harder to wake me from the daydream.

This was my job, my first opportunity to prove myself, and I refused to risk it all before it could even begin.

As if he could sense my frustration through the wavelengths of the earth, I received a text.

Did you get your contract? - B$

BS is right...

I climbed out of bed, trying not to wake Landon as I headed to the living room to reply.

Kennedy: I did.

Any questions? - B$

In all honesty, nothing had stood out besides that one little thing. In fact, Bryson had set terms that were better than I could've imagined. I thought about just saying no and pretending like I hadn't even seen the part that was lingering in my head. But that would've been me punking out as always, so I replied with my true thoughts.

Kennedy: Umm... what's up with this whole consensual sex thing? Isn't that unethical?

I waited a few long, anxious moments before multiple texts came through.

No. Unethical is trying to sue for doing something we both enjoyed... thoroughly. - B$

It's just a protection, that's all. - B$

No pun intended. ;) - B$

Crap.

Why had I even said anything?

After the night before, I knew it didn't take much for me to get out of character when it came to Bryson. So how I had managed to set myself up for failure even though he wasn't physically present was beyond me.

If I was single, I probably would've came up with something slick to say back. Something that hinted at,

"I'm feeling you too." But that was hardly the case, so I texted back like a regular employee.

Kennedy: Understood.

I was just getting ready to go back to bed and check on Landon until my phone vibrated in my hand again.

Great. See you later. ;) - B$

I stopped in the middle of the hallway, immediately flashing over to his email to make sure I hadn't missed any plans or meetings. When I saw there was nothing and couldn't think of anything he or Leslie had mentioned off the top of my head, I replied back.

Kennedy: Later? What's later?

His response came quick.

I'm taking you to dinner to celebrate you accepting the position. - B$

No way.

There was no way I could let Bryson - *my boss, be damned* - take me to dinner. Dinner was way too intimate of a setting to even think about having to survive a whole one alone with him.

Kennedy: You really don't have to do that, Bryson.

I want to. - B$

I sighed, trying to come up with a way out. It wasn't really a good look to skip out on getting to know my boss which would more than likely give me better insight on his personal style.

But dinner?

Kennedy: Can we do lunch instead?

At least with lunch, it would be light outside. And since Landon had plans to grade papers all afternoon, going to lunch with my boss wouldn't sound too sketchy. In fact, he'd probably be proud of me for even mentioning willingly doing something social.

That works too. I'll send a car around 1. Wear something casual. - B$

Bryson

I was desperate to see where her head was at.

Her texts weren't giving enough for me to be able to tell if she was picking up on my little hints; if she was feeling the vibe that *I* felt when I was around her. It hardly seemed possible that I had only met her yesterday, but I suppose that helped explain why I couldn't get her off of my mind.

Kennedy was gorgeous.

She knew that and I knew that, so of course I wanted to fuck her.

Well... actually, I take that back.

Kennedy wasn't the type of girl I could just have sex with and toss to the side. Kennedy was the type of girl I wanted to wine and dine, come up with some corny ass jokes to tell her just to see her smile. The type of girl I wanted sitting courtside at my games before I brought her home for some slow, long love-making to celebrate.

She deserved the bubble bath, strawberries, and champagne treatment; not the quickie in the backseat kind. And from what I could tell about her, she wasn't exactly the type to get down like that anyway. I mean, even the fact that she wanted to do lunch instead of dinner showed me she was willing to duck and dodge the pleasure to focus on the business. But I had something in store to test her willpower.

I was sure she wasn't expecting to have lunch at my crib, but I figured it was a good place to start getting to know each other.

For the job, that is.

The doorbell rang signaling her arrival and I licked my lips, excited to see what her reaction to me was going to be. I pulled the door open and got an even better reaction than I could've imagined. Her eyes slowly scanned my exposed body, right down to the towel wrapped around my waist.

"Up here, Kennedy," I teased.

Her mocha brown skin turned rosy as she put her hands over her face. *"Oh. Oh! I'm... wow.* Can we start over?"

I laughed as I pulled her inside by the hand, shutting the door behind us. Then I gave her the same onceover she had already given me, quickly learning that her idea of dressing casual was totally different than anything I could've thought of. She made her skin-tight jeans and thigh-high boots, with a sequined blazer thrown over a plain tee look fresh out of someone's print Ad. But considering her occupation, I suppose I should've been more specific.

"Well, welcome to my house."

She looked straight up at my vaulted ceilings as she asked, "You live in this humongous house all by yourself?"

I shrugged. "For now; yeah. Just waiting for the right woman to turn it into a home I guess."

She flashed her eyes at me like I had said something crazy, but it was the God honest truth regardless of how it may have sounded to her. Having whatever girl I wanted, when I wanted her was getting old. And after falling out with the girl I saw as the closest thing to "right", a replacement sounded better than ever.

"Makes sense. Now can we talk about why you're in a towel?"

Easy access.

"I figured I'd give you your first test. To dress me, that is."

She didn't flinch as she answered, "Oh. Okay. Well where's your closet?"

"In the bedroom."

Still no flinching.

"O... kay. So where's your bedroom?"

"Upstairs," I said with a flirtatious smile to test her. She only returned my smile with a politer one as she said, "Lead the way."

She followed me up the stairs and I paused at the door of my master suite to ask, "You ready to see where the magic happens?"

"Very funny, Bryson. Come on before you catch a cold being out here all naked."

"Well, I'm not *all* naked. But I can definitely make that happen if that's what you prefer."

There's the flinch.

She gulped before she pushed out, "Towel is fine. Let's get to the closet."

I opened the door and allowed her to step in first so I could get a good view of her ass.

Damn, I shouldn't have done that.

My towel did nothing to hide my natural, bodily reaction to a fine ass woman being in my bedroom.

She looked around with wide eyes as she said, "Wow. This is amazing, Bryson. You actually have pretty good taste."

I walked over to the closet with Kennedy in tow, turning on the light as I replied, "I wish I could take the credit, but I have to give that to Leslie's wife. She's an interior designer."

She was already sorting through my clothes but stopped once she realized what I had said. "Wait a minute. Leslie's a...?"

"Lesbian? Yeah. She finds you just as sexy as I do."
She brushed off my little compliment as she replied,
"Wow. I never would've guessed that one."

I leaned against the center island of drawers as I
asked, "What? That I find you sexy as hell?"

Her voice was low as she answered, "No. I guessed
that."

I couldn't help but tease, "Ohhhh, so I got a little
cocky one on my hands?"

She refused to give me her eyes, instead focusing on
the clothes as she responded, "Not at all. I just hear you,
even when you don't think I do."

"So you're just ignoring me?"

"No. I'm..." she paused, letting her head fall into my
shirts that were hung on the top rack of my closet before
she continued, "Bryson, I told you already. I'm engaged."

So I wasn't hearing things last night. It really
should've been no surprise that Kennedy was taken. All
the good ones were usually off the market. But I had to
take a peek at her hand again before I asked, "If you're
engaged, why aren't you wearing a ring?"

"It's... I don't know." She resumed her job of
finding me an outfit as she said, "I keep forgetting to put
it on. Still not used to the whole thing."

"Ah, so it's a new engagement. How long have you
guys been together?"

She answered short and direct, "A year and a half."

"Not even two years and he already popped the
question? You must have some bomb ass pussy."

She yanked a shirt down, causing the hanger to fly
off the rack as she said, "Excuse me?"

I challenged her, taking the few steps over to where
she stood. "That's the only way you could've locked him
down that fast. Bomb ass pussy, bomb ass head game..."

"Bomb ass personality?! Jesus, you can't possibly be

30

this shallow." She stepped away angrily, going to the side of the closet my pants were kept.

"I was just joking with you, Kennedy. Relax."

"Whatever. Here, throw this on."

She tossed me the shirt she had pulled down and a pair of jeans from across the room. I dropped my towel right in front of her just for shits and giggles and you would've thought she saw a ghost.

She didn't turn away, instead choosing to cover her eyes with her hands as she screeched, "Bryson! What do you think you're doing?!"

I shrugged, trying to hold back my laugh as I said, "I'm getting dressed, Kennedy. Throwing on some clothes like you told me to."

"You could've at least let me get out of here first."

Though that was probably true, I had no problem reminding her, "Kennedy, you're engaged to be married. If you only have eyes for your future husband, you shouldn't be worried about my dick, right?"

She could only sigh, knowing I was right. So instead of arguing the facts, she insisted, "Just... give me a warning next time, please."

Kennedy

Lunch with Bryson was... *nice.*

Though after seeing his dick, I hardly imagined things getting anywhere near back to normal. But they had in a way that made me excited about working with him. He wasn't always the sexually-charged, cocky jock-type that he appeared to be. He was actually a decent guy, with a more than positive outlook on life.

The time had flown by. And since it was getting relatively late and I knew Landon would be checking in soon, I decided to head home. Bryson looked a little disappointed when I told him, like he didn't want me to go. But I knew for my own sake it was mandatory.

We stood at the door together as I waited for the driver to pull up.

"Considering what you usually wear, I'm surprised you had so many gems in your closet," I teased.

His eyes bore into mine as he replied, "So you're one of those passive types, huh? The kind that gives slick, little backhanded compliments?"

"Contrary to popular belief, every woman doesn't fall into a category. Some women simply don't unveil every personality trait the first couple of times they meet someone. *Some of us...* some of us like to keep things a mystery until the friendship develops. You know, allow things to unfold."

"So basically what you're saying is you're an undercover freak."

How in the world...?!

"What?! No! That's not what I'm saying at all."

He smirked as he said, "All I heard was unlike most women, you keep your legs closed until you're comfortable with someone. Is that accurate?"

How do I answer this without cussing him out or sounding ridiculous?

"As true as that may be, that's still not what I said. And how did we even get to that? We were talking about your wardrobe."

He flashed me one of his panty-wetting smiles as he said, "My mind tends to deviate when I'd prefer another topic. I apologize."

I tried not to appear too amused, offering him a smile that only held half of his enthusiasm as I changed the subject. "Well I appreciate the hospitality and you showing me your closet. I have a pretty good idea of how we should move forward, what things we need to add, and what God-awful things we need to get rid of. So just send me your schedule and we can plan for the week accordingly."

He gave me a nod as he replied, "Will do."

Before I could get away, he pulled me into a hug that felt so like home I began to relax. With his arms slung against my waist, he gave me a little kiss to my forehead like we were old friends and had done this a million times.

Kennedy, what are you doing?!

I pulled away in disbelief that things had even gotten to that point so fast. But looking at Bryson with his guilty little smirk told me exactly why I had become so vulnerable.

I had to be more careful.

"Hey babe. I'm making your favorite."

I found Landon in the kitchen wearing only an apron and sweatpants slung low against his waist as he stirred his famous homemade sauce on the stove. Between that and the fresh flowers on the counter with a card tucked in the middle, the guilt of spending time with Bryson hit me clean in the chest.

I'm a terrible fiancée.

"*Wow.* It smells so good. But I'm not really hungry. Had a big lunch." I even put a hand to my stomach to emphasize how full I was.

He kept stirring as he tossed over his shoulder, "Oh yeah? How'd that go?"

I tried to sound nonchalant as I responded, "It went well. Got a good idea of his wardrobe so we can start building a better one."

He turned the sauce down, wiping his hands with a towel before pulling me slung against his body and telling me, "I'm so proud of you." Then he sealed his praises with a kiss, the familiarity of his lips resonating with my soul.

Before I could lean in for a second dose, my phone vibrated against the counter. I peeked over Landon's shoulder to see the message before I was forced to push it to the ground. I just knew my screen was cracked, but that was small scale compared to the disaster that could've happened if Landon had seen what popped up.

He slowly looked down to the ground at my sacrificed phone. "Aww damn, how'd that happen?"

I shrugged, acting surprised as if I hadn't done the damage myself. "I don't know. I guess it just vibrated right off the counter."

My little white lie actually worked as he replied, "Well I know a few people that fix electronics on the side at the school. Want me to take it in when I get off work tomorrow?"

"NO! I mean… *no*, it's fine. I'll do it. I have time in the morning."

He smiled, giving me another kiss as he said, "Whatever you say, babe."

I licked my lips as I watched him take off his apron, revealing his perfectly sculpted chest and v-shaped abs as he tossed it on the counter. Landon was as fine as they came, a sight for sore eyes really. But I'd be damned if my mind wasn't on the picture message I was forced to destroy my phone over.

Bryson

I laid in bed anxious for a reply.

I wasn't sure what her reaction would be, but I knew she wasn't just going to act like she didn't get it. I mean, having a naked picture of me *would* give her a better idea of my body structure and how to dress it accordingly, so I was really doing her a favor.

At least, that was my halfway decent excuse for sending it.

The response finally came in. But instead of the one I expected, there were multiple.

Kennedy: What the fuck do you think you're doing?!

Kennedy: If this is how it's gonna be, I can't work for you.

Kennedy: Matter of fact, just give me a good reference so I can find another job.

I smiled at my phone, finding it hilarious how riled up she was over a little picture. She was usually so cool, calm and collected. So to see her even use an expletive was enough for me to recognize that the picture had, indeed, done its job.

LOL. I'm sorry, Kennedy. I was just being silly. -B$

Her response came quick.

Kennedy: Well your silly ass just caused me to break my phone.

Squeezed it too hard while you were gettin' one off? ;) - B$

Kennedy: No. Pushed it to the floor to prevent

you from getting your ass kicked by my fiancé.
He don't want those problems. - B$
Kennedy: Not. The. Point. Just don't do it again.
I mean, EVER again.
Understood. - B$
Then it dawned on me.
*How are you texting me if your phone is broken? -
B$*
Kennedy: Computer. iMessage.
Is he there? Can he see your screen? - B$
I could tell she was typing by the little dots that
appeared.
Kennedy: Yeah, he's here. But no, he can't. Put
'em to sleep. Bomb ass pussy for the win. ;)
LOL! So you can say it, but I can't? - B$
Kennedy: I'll see you later this week, Bryson.
Good night.
I could imagine her smile as I replied with a smile of
my own.
Night, Kennedy. - B$

"So... how soon will we be interviewing for a new
stylist?"
I plopped down on a chair in front of Leslie's desk,
putting my feet on top of it even though I knew she hated
when I did it.
"What are you talking about?"
She wore a sly grin as she said, "Come on, Bryson. I
know you better than you know yourself. I saw the way
you were looking at Kennedy. And I'm sure you've
already tried to pull the ol' dinner and chill move."
Damn, she really does know me.
Instead of confirming her knowledge, I tossed out

the only relevant information. "She's engaged."

At first she brushed it off with a, "Yeah right." But I stared at her for a few moments longer before she caught my drift. "Wait. You're serious, aren't you?"

I nodded my head. "I'm serious."

"Well I didn't see a ring on her finger."

"Me neither, but it's true. I saw it on her *Facebook* page. *Future Mrs. Montgomery.*"

Her dude looked as square as they came, but I really shouldn't have been surprised. Of course somebody as bomb as Kennedy would be engaged to a damn school teacher.

"Did she have an engagement picture as her profile picture?"

"No."

"A picture with her ring and the caption, *"I said yes"*?"

"No."

"Pictures from the proposal?"

"No."

She put her elbows on the desk, letting her head rest on her palm as she said, "Damn. So she's not excited about it. Any girl who's excited about their impending nuptials has at least one of the three."

"So what's that supposed to mean?"

"It means…" The pregnant pause had me completely tuned in by the time she continued, "It doesn't mean anything, Bryson. I'm just fuckin' with your hopes." Then she busted out laughing like she was at a damn comedy show, instantly pissing me off.

"Yo, that's not funny."

"You should've saw your face, though! You were all into it like I was gonna tell you to go after the girl even though she's engaged. What kind of person would I be to encourage that bullshit?"

I understood exactly where she was coming from even though I wasn't ready to admit it.

"I don't know, Leslie. It's weird, though. Like I know she's taken, but *I can't*... I can't stop thinking about her. And not even about sex. Like I really wanna get to know her." Though she seemed pretty normal on the surface, Kennedy's little hints of a spicy personality had me intrigued like no other.

Leslie stood up, grabbing a stress ball as she paced back and forth next to her desk. "This sounds a little too much like that Alexis girl. I mean, she was in a relationship too. But you acted like it didn't exist, even when you were in a relationship of your own."

Damn, she's always right.

"I know, I know. I'm trippin'."

She nodded to agree. "Yes, you are. And Kennedy seems like a good girl, Bryson. Don't ruin her."

"*Ruin her?* If anything, she's gonna ruin me."

She sighed. "Bryson, just keep it professional. *Please.*"

I looked away, knowing it was a little too late for that. Leslie immediately picked up on my reaction and asked, "What did you do?"

I closed my eyes before I admitted, "I sent her a nude."

Leslie squeezed the stress ball so hard I was just sure it was going to pop. "Gotdamnit, Bryson! Who do you think you are? God's gift to women? Nobody wants to see your naked ass all the time."

I wouldn't take it that far, but my nudes were certainly more of a treat than a trick.

"Just because you don't, doesn't mean she didn't."

She rolled her eyes. "Your logic is all fucked up, you know that? Gosh, how did I get stuck with such a shitty client?"

—

40

I brushed her off. "Oh, Leslie. You know I'm your favorite. Don't play." Even though Leslie acted like she didn't like me more often than not, I knew she had a soft spot for my antics.

"Yeah, you're my favorite because you make me the most money. Other than that, I can't stand your black ass."

I quickly countered, "That's racist."

She gave me a death stare as she stated the obvious. "I'm black too, asshole."

"Still racist," I replied with a smirk just to annoy her.

She rolled her eyes again. "Go find some business, Bryson. Don't you have practice soon?"

I took my feet from her desk so I could stand up and get going. "Yep. Then I'm meeting up with Kennedy to go shopping."

"*A shopping date*? Gag me."

She stuck her finger in her mouth, but I couldn't help teasing her, "With what? A dil..."

She cut me off, pointing to the door. "Out! Bye! Be gone!"

I laughed my way out of the door before tossing over my shoulder, "Love you too, Leslie."

Kennedy

"Bryson, you can *not* be serious."

I waited for his expression to change, but he didn't budge.

"These are dope, Kenn. I don't understand why you don't like them."

Seeing a grown ass man in overalls wasn't exactly my idea of "dope". But Bryson claimed that ever since he saw one of his boys pull off the look, he had to have a pair. I didn't even know they made overalls that large, but leave it to him to actually find a pair.

I attempted to put things in perspective, hoping he'd actually listen. "They're dope if you're like twelve. And a girl. Not for a multi-millionaire professional basketball player. So put them back."

He gave the fakest little pout as he said, "You're mean."

I almost got offended, but then I realized who I was dealing with - *Mr. Jokester himself.*

"I'm not mean, I'm honest. And I take my visions seriously. So put them back."

He crossed his arms over his chest, still challenging me, "It's my money. I can buy them if I want to."

"Of course you can. But is that *really* the point of my job? I can go home and find somebody else to work for if…" It was already the third time I had to threaten him, but luckily he had cut me off every time.

"Fine, hard ass. I'll put them back. *For now.*"

I wore a pleased smile as I told him, "Thank you."

Then I returned to skimming through the rows of clothes in the private designer boutique, trying my hardest to stay in the men's section instead of venturing to the women's like I really wanted to do. I had always dreamed of shopping for myself in one of these fancy little places, but could never afford it. And unfortunately, that was still the case.

"What about these, Kennedy? Do these meet your standards?"

I cocked my head to the side, putting my hand to my chin as I thought about what I could do with the sleek leather pants he was holding up. I knew the whole "fitted" look was in for men. And with Bryson's already lengthy frame, the pants would certainly do him justice.

"I like those. You can keep them."

He looked satisfied as he tossed them over his shoulder and went back to looking for more. I was honestly surprised by how patient he was being with the whole process; hardly irritated by the fact that we were already an hour in and hadn't gathered much to purchase.

Landon would've surely dragged me out of the store by now.

I grabbed a few things from the rack before I found Bryson looking at the shoes. "Here. Go try these on."

He flipped through the shirts, handing one back to me. "I'll try *these* on. This one isn't gonna work."

Though the shirt was one of my favorites, I was willing to sacrifice it for the moment. "Compromise. *Fine.* Now go try them on. I'll be out here."

He gave me a skeptical look before I urged him on with a push.

As I waited for him to come out of the dressing room, I checked my newly fixed phone and saw I had a text.

Mr. Montgomery: Hey babe. I hope you're

having a good day. The kids are bouncing off the walls. Must be a full moon. Anyway, I can't wait to see you tonight. Love you. ;)

I smiled into my phone until I felt eyes hovering over my shoulder.

"Aww, isn't that sweet? He can't wait to see you tonight, Kennedy," Bryson said in a mocking tone.

I tossed my phone into my purse, turning around to fix the collar of his button-up shirt. "Nosy much?"

"Nah. More like, jealous much."

I took a step back, pretending to observe his outfit, though my mind was racing after his little admission. I tried to keep my tone level as I asked, "*Jealous*? Jealous why?"

"Jealous that I'm not the one making you smile like that."

I took a step forward to adjust his shirt a little more. "You know... you could always find yourself a special girl to make smile like that. I'm just sure they're lined up waiting for their shot at a ball player."

He stopped me from my meddling, grabbing me by the wrists to get my attention. "It's funny that that's always the assumption. But the truth is, as much fun as that offers temporarily, there's nothing like having a real one to call your own."

"Damn, girl. You're fuckin' me like a porn star..."

I heard Landon talking, but I could hardly interpret what he was saying as I took out every ounce of sexual tension I had built up during the day on his dick. Of course we had sex on the regular, but I'd be damned if I didn't feel like I needed it more than ever tonight.

After spending the whole day with Bryson under his

45

watchful, flirtatious eye, I was more than ready to get home to my man. He hadn't been in the house for more than five minutes before I pounced on him, desperate for a fix. But even more so, desperate to remind myself why I was with him.

Starting with his dick...

"Fuck! Right there, baby. *Right...*" I shuddered as I came harder than ever before, collapsing on top of him while he continued to pump into me to get his own.

"Shit!"

I could feel him oozing inside of me, his essence filling me up in a way I had never let any other man do before. I rolled off of him as I tried to catch my breath.

"Damn, Kennedy. What the hell was that all about?"

"I umm... I missed you today. That's all."

"Well can you miss me more often?" he asked with a goofy little laugh as he turned me on my side to spoon me, not even bothering to at least let me clean myself up first.

I sighed, scooting deeper into the curve of his body while I tried to come up with a response. Of course I had missed Landon; I always missed Landon when we were apart. But did that *really* explain the super boost of sexual energy that came over me the second he walked through the door? Or was it the....

Stop it, Kennedy!

This is your fiancé.

Of course it's because of him.

Instead of answering his question, I asked one of my own. "Did you... miss me?"

"Of course I missed you, babe. And I'll miss you even more tomorrow. And the next day. And the next day." He punctuated his lines with kisses that in the moment should've soothed me, but I was too wrapped up in what he had said.

———

46

Tomorrow.

Tomorrow, I'd be spending most of the day and night with the ever-draining Bryson; first getting him dressed for his afternoon game and postgame conference, then getting his wardrobe ready for the movie premiere he was attending out in LA the day after that, along with whatever *Instagram* model he had decided to take.

Waist-training, detox tea drinking ass...

Stop it, Kenn...

"Kennedy, are you alright? It seems like something is on your mind."

See what you did?!

I tried not to sound panicky as I replied, "No, I'm fine. I was just... thinking about what kind of outfit I wanted to put Bryson's date in tomorrow."

Partially true...

"Oh, he has a girlfriend? *Phew.* That's a relief."

Not having to ask him face-to-face made it easier to inquire, "Why do you say that?"

He used the tip of his finger to draw lazy circles around my nipple as he explained, "No man is excited about having his woman work exclusively with another man, no matter how famous he is. But since he has a girlfriend, I don't have anything to worry about."

Even though I knew the girl wasn't *exactly* his girlfriend, letting Landon believe that would certainly keep me out of trouble.

"You didn't have anything to worry about regardless, Landon."

Partially true...

"Oh I know... *Mrs. Montgomery.*"

I'd be damned if I didn't cringe on the inside before correcting him, "*Almost* Mrs. Montgomery."

"*Future* Mrs. Montgomery," he tossed back, letting his hand glide from my breasts down my belly to my

---

folds that were still saturated from round one. "Mmm... I see she's ready for me again."

In all honesty, I really just wanted to go to sleep so I could be fresh-faced for the next day. But the idea of Bryson doing this same thing with his little date tomorrow gave me a sudden surge of energy.

Bryson

"Where's whatsherface?"

I could tell Kennedy had a little attitude about her the second she showed up to my house, though I couldn't figure out why. She seemed fine this morning when she picked out my clothes for the game. But now that she was looking through the recently delivered racks of women's clothing, her whole demeanor had switched. You would've thought the clothes had done her wrong with how aggressively she was sorting through them.

I watched her closely as I told her, "She's on her way. I set her up with a bunch of appointments to get all freshened up for the trip." I figured it was the least I could do since I hadn't given her much attention other than the occasional heart eyes emoji in the comments of her *Instagram* pictures. But all it took was that and a few DMs to convince her to join me for the weekend.

She yanked a dress from the rack, laying it on the couch as she tossed out, *"Hmph. Must be nice."*

I watched her for a few moments longer as she opened a box of *Louboutin* pumps, staring at them in awe before closing it and setting it next to the dress.

"You like those?"

She shot me a glare. "Is that even a real question?"

I walked over to the couch, opening the box myself and pulling one of the shoes out as I tried to figure out what was so special about them. I mean, they were just shoes.

"What's up with you women and designer shoes

anyway? Most of us guys would rather have you barefoot and preg…"

She cut me off. "Nope. Nope. Nope. Not gonna go there. Not falling into that trap."

She made herself busy straightening out the dress she had picked out for my date as I took a step closer and pried deeper. "Let me guess. You're one of those, *My body, my cho…*"

She held a hand up to stop me again. "Bryson, stop while you're ahead. Please."

I stepped right behind her, tempted to wrap my arms around her waist as I teased, "Why stop me? I'm on a roll and you know it."

She stepped to her left to respond, "No. All you're *doing* is undermining the potential of women by acting like they don't have the power."

I found her again, this time stepping in front of her the second she turned around. "All the power is in the pussy. You and I both know that."

Her eyes were fixated on mine and there was no denying the flicker of interest. I licked my lips ready to make a move, but she spoke again. "My pussy may be powerful, but it's not all I'm worth."

"So it's bomb then, huh?" I teased.

She rolled her eyes, stepping away to reply, "That's none of your business."

I filled the gap once again, this time unable to keep my hands to myself as I wrapped my arms around her thin waist. "What if I make it my business?"

She rested her hands on my chest, giving me a little push just as the doorbell rang. "*Your* business… is waiting for you at the door."

I didn't really want to go answer it; wanted to savor this moment of lighthearted back and forth banter with Kennedy. But when the doorbell rang again and I looked

—

50

down to her left hand that was still near my chest, I knew this was as good as it was going to get.

"I don't like it."

I threw my hands up as Monica turned down yet another one of Kennedy's masterpieces. We had been at it for what felt like hours as we tried to find something for her to wear to the movie premiere, but nothing seemed to please her.

That CoverGirl contract from a few years back must've went straight to her head.

I tried to hide my annoyance as I told her, "Monica, if you keep this up, we'll miss our flight. Just pick something."

She whined, "It's not that simple, Bryson. I have an image to protect."

Out of my peripheral, I saw Kennedy roll her eyes. But she kept quiet, sifting through the racks for yet another option.

"You weren't thinking about your image when you posted all those thirst traps on *Instagram*. So why are you so worried about it now?"

She had the nerve to get an attitude as if I was lying. "Excuse me! Those were for my brand."

"Could've fooled me…"

Kennedy stopped to smile before she went back to the rack.

"Well maybe if you got a *real* stylist in here, we wouldn't have this problem."

Oh shit.

I heard the distinct click of hangers smashing together before Kennedy said, "The stylist doesn't bring the outfit to life, the person who's wearing it does. So

51

maybe you need to check yourself before you worry about *my* credentials."

I hardly expected to see Kennedy clap back, but I was honestly impressed. Hell, that shit actually turned me on. But instead of focusing on that, I had to set the record straight. "Kennedy's right, Monica. You can either pick one of the options she's already laid out for you, or just stay your ass here cause I'm done going back and forth about this."

She looked ready to argue back, but I dared her with my eyes to say something. So instead she only growled, throwing her hands down as she said, "Fine! I'll take this dress and this... ensemble."

"And tell her thank you."

Now both women were looking at me.

Monica's was wearing a scowl as she asked, "What?"

"Tell Kennedy thank you for picking out these wonderful options for you to choose from. She did you a favor, ya know."

Monica acted like the idea was crazy, brushing me off as she said, "Bryson, you have got to be kidding me."

"Didn't your mama raise you with any manners? I mean, you wouldn't be able to tell from that booty pic you posted, but..."

That got her attention.

"Thank you, Kennedy." She said it so low I could hardly hear her.

I thought about making her repeat herself until Kennedy replied, "You're welcome."

Kennedy

Took a shift at the club. I'll be back before sunrise. Love, Hubby :).

I sighed at the note that was attached to a new floral arrangement, smaller than usual but still perfect in taste. Though I wished Landon would stop pulling shifts at that damn strip club, I couldn't help but acknowledge how perfect he was. Handsome as all get out, provider by nature, socially-conscious career, good with kids, could cook almost better than me; everything you could ask for in a husband.

But my mind was beyond occupied with the devil himself.

I felt crazy as hell for even allowing my thoughts of him to get so intense, but it was like there was nothing I could do to fight it; especially after spending more time with him. The more time I spent, the deeper I fell into a trap I had no business even being around.

Get it together, Kennedy.

I changed out of my clothes into pajamas, hoping there wasn't even a hint of Bryson's intoxicating scent from the multiple hugs he tried to justify before he headed to the airport with his little chick. I sniffed my shirt just to check, and sure enough there it was. All freshly-showered, and manly, *and...* I tossed it into the laundry basket before I could melt.

I felt so stupid for being even remotely attracted to Bryson. I mean, he was fine, sure... and rich. and...

Did I say fine already?

But other than that he was a misogynist, he was arrogant, and he just assumed every girl would give up the goodies to him because of his stature. It was pathetic, really, that all that caramel, tattooed fineness was going to waste on such a... *dog.*

That's exactly what Bryson was.

A damn dog.

And you're getting ready to marry a real man in Landon.

Instead of staying in my thoughts, I went to the bathroom to brush my teeth, wash my face, and tie my hair for the night. Then I snuggled in bed with my laptop so I could fall asleep to something on *Netflix.*

It didn't take long before my head was nodding off and my eyes were glazing over. I was just getting ready to throw in the towel and shut my computer when it began to ring, signaling an incoming *FaceTime* call.

Bryson Harris.

I panicked, first looking down at my chest that had been braless since I came home, then touching my head that was covered in a scarf, and finally adjusting my glasses that I only wore at night when I was tired of my contacts.

I can't let him see me like this!

I pulled my scarf from my head, brushing my hair down with my fingers before hitting the key to answer the call. Once it connected, I could tell he was already in bed too, his chest tattoos on full display and his durag tied tight.

Fine. Ass.

His smile was pleasant as he said, "Hey you."

I tried to clear my throat before I addressed him. "Bryson. What's going on? Is something wrong?" Considering it was well past two in the morning, that was the only logical explanation for the call.

—

54

His bare muscles flexed as he laughed. "Nothing's wrong. I just wanted to... talk to you."

Talk to me?

He's on a weekend getaway and wanted to "talk to me"?

"Where's Monica?"

"Man, I ditched her the second we landed. That girl was gettin' on my gotdamn nerves."

I couldn't help but laugh considering I had been thinking the same thing once she showed up to his house, though I was actually grateful when she did show up as Bryson was getting a little too close for me to control.

"Makes sense. Well now who are you going to take?" I was sure it was far from slim-pickings for him, even last minute.

"That's actually why I was calling. I wanted to see if you would... fly out and come with me."

My heart leaped from my chest.

It was flattering as hell that he had even thought to invite me, but... "Bryson, no. Come on now." I was already spending more than enough time with him. And joining him on his trip was hardly necessary.

"Why not? And don't say because it's late notice."

"How about because I have a fiancé? Engaged people don't go on dates. You do realize that, right?" I always thought stuff like that was common knowledge, but apparently not.

He brushed me off. "Oh, Kennedy. Save that shit. If you were *really* engaged, you wouldn't have answered my call at this hour."

I shouldn't have...

"No. If you respected my engagement, you wouldn't be *calling* at this hour. But you're my boss. I have to answer." I really hated how much power he had in this situation, especially after our earlier conversation.

———

He smiled as if he was having an epiphany before he said, "Well as your boss, I'm telling you to get your ass to LA ASAP."

The panic returned. There was no way in hell I was going to fly out to LA just to… please Bryson.

"Bryson, that's not fair and you know it."

He challenged me, "I'll respect your engagement if you respect me as your boss."

"Bryson…"

His goofy little smile returned. "I'll send you the flight information in a minute. See you tomorrow, Kennedy."

&

The flight from Philly to Los Angeles wasn't long enough.

In fact, no amount of time would've prepared me for the last-minute flight out at Bryson's request. It was like even though he and I both knew I shouldn't be here, he made it his mission to test every inch of my moral capacity.

I sighed just thinking about it as I dragged my carry-on bag through the terminals before making my way towards the pick-up area where a driver was supposed to be waiting for me. But instead, I only found Bryson's tall frame terribly disguised in a hoodie, baseball cap, and sunglasses. I suppose since people were used to seeing celebrities in this particular airport, his presence wasn't that big of a deal. But his effort to hide himself was humorous at best. He even held a sign with my name on it as if I wouldn't recognize him.

"Kennedy! Over here!"

I rolled my eyes as I approached him. "You don't really think you're incognito, do you?"

"Shhh! Come on before they figure it out."

I laughed as he took my bag and lead me outside to where a car was waiting.

After handing my bag off to the real chauffeur, he opened the door for me, letting me climb in first then following. We rode off in silence as I watched the city pass us by through the window.

"So how was your flight out?"

"It was fine. Oh! I need to call Landon and tell him I made it." Though he wasn't too enthused about the last-minute trip, he still understood it being part of the job.

"That's his name? Landon... Montgomery, right?"

I finally turned his way.

"Yeah. How'd you know that?" I asked as I dialed Landon's number and pressed call.

"Uh... background checks. We had to know everything about you before we put you on."

"Right." I held up my hand to put Bryson on hold just as Landon picked up.

"Hey babe... Yeah, I made it safe and sound... Okay, I'll keep in touch... Yes, I promise, Landon... Okay... Okay, love you too. Bye."

I could feel Bryson's eyes all over me as I pressed end, prompting me to ask, "What?"

His face was stern as he said, "Give me your phone."

"What?" I asked again for new reasons.

"Give me your phone. You won't need it."

Okay, this dude is trippin'.

"Bryson, I'm not giving you my phone. That's ridiculous and you know it." Between keeping in touch with Landon, emergencies, and social media, there was no way I was handing over my pride and joy.

"Just listen to me, Kennedy. I'll give it back in the morning. I promise."

I eyed him for a long time, trying to figure out his

motive. Maybe he expected his company to be present instead of wrapped up in the virtual world. Or maybe he just… expected a certain level of privacy in situations like this.

That, I could respect.

I powered my phone off and handed it over, watching as he put it in the pocket of his sweatpants like it was his own.

"Thatta girl. Now let's have some fun."

Bryson

I was out of control.

I always kind of felt like my ducks were in a row no matter how it looked from the outside, but something about Kennedy had me feeling completely reckless. It was like I knew exactly what I was doing, but I had no idea what I was doing at the same time. I mean, I knew I had some control since I was the one who signed her checks. But I knew I didn't have any control when it came to my attraction to her.

She was a taken woman.

And yet, the inkling of hope I felt with every twinkle in her eye when she was around me kept me intrigued enough to test the limits.

Leslie would probably kill me if she knew what was happening.

I sat on the couch in the living room of our suite, the only common area we'd have to share since our bedrooms were on opposite sides. Kennedy insisted on taking a shower to freshen up after the flight, so I was stuck waiting for her to finish with a hard-on from thinking about her fine ass naked.

Though it was muffled, I could hear her singing her little heart out in the bathroom. The song sounded familiar, but I couldn't figure it out right away. So I got up and took the couple of steps towards her bathroom door.

Since the door wasn't locked, I went inside to get an even better listen. I made myself comfortable against the counter as I vibed to her perfect harmony while she sang about wanting someone in her world but already being someone else's girl.

I looked over near the sink and noticed a pile of lacy undergarments.

Damn, is this for me?

I was holding the panties in the air, already imagining them against her perfect mocha skin as I heard, "Bryson! What are you doing in here?!"

My eyes flashed over to her unfortunately already toweled frame. "My bad. I… heard you singing. What were you singing?"

She snatched off her shower cap as she asked, "You heard me singing? You came in here and picked up my panties because you heard me singing? You can do better than that, Bryson."

"No. These just distracted me from my original mission. But I really did come in here to figure out what you were singing. So what was it?"

Her eyes casted towards her toes that were painted a bright pink. "*Next Lifetime.* Erykah Badu."

"I knew it sounded familiar! *That was…* that was my mom's favorite song before she passed away." I could vividly remember her singing the tune as she cleaned the house every Sunday. It went Kirk Franklin, then Yolanda Adams, and then Erykah Badu like clockwork.

"*Oh.* I'm sorry to hear that, Bryson."

She gave me the same empathetic smile I had gotten used to receiving from just about everyone over the years. I don't know why people always went to feeling sorry for me like I wasn't doing well for myself after the fact. I mean, I had made it to the league, was Rookie of the Year, won a championship. I was doing everything my mother ever envisioned for me. If anything, people should've been happy to see me accomplish so much.

—

So I brushed her off the same way I had done everyone else. "No worries, Kennedy. She's in a better place now."

"Well can you get out of here so I can get dressed?"

"You saw me naked. Why can't I see you?" I said, only halfway teasing.

"Bryson... *out!*"

"Bryson!"

"B-Money, over here!"

"Bryson!"

The cameras were flashing left and right as I crossed the red carpet. I smiled for as many as my cheeks allowed before taking a break to answer a couple of questions from the reporters.

"Bryson, are you excited for the movie?"

"Bryson, is the season meeting your expectations?"

"Bryson, who'd you bring tonight?"

I looked over to Kennedy who was off mixing and mingling with some of the other attendees. I was proud as I watched her exchange business cards with a couple of the publicists for other celebrities, but I knew there was no way I was letting her get away already.

She was mine.

I mean... she was *my* stylist.

Exclusively.

But since she was an up-and-comer and I knew it wasn't realistic for me to expect to keep her in the position forever, I decided to shine a light on her.

"I brought my stylist. Killed two birds with one stone," I said with a rehearsed laugh. I knew Kennedy couldn't hear me with all the hoopla surrounding us, but somehow she still turned my way at that exact moment.

—

"So are you two dating?"

I gave her a onceover, causing her to blush and hating the partial-truth of my answer. "She's... *engaged.* But she's been dying to see this movie ever since I mentioned the premiere to her, so her fiancé gave her a pass for the night."

"Aww! What a nice guy! Enjoy the movie, Bryson!"

I gave the reporter a nod before waving Kennedy over to join me. She smiled, offering goodbyes to her newfound friends, then headed my way.

As soon as she crossed the carpet, the cameras began to flash the same way they had for me. But it caught Kennedy completely off-guard, causing her to stumble a little before holding her hand up to block the flashing lights.

Instinctively, I grabbed her by the hand, dragging her to safety. I didn't let her go before I had the chance to ask, "Are you okay?"

She pulled her hand out of my hold as she answered. "Yeah. Yeah, I'm fine."

She straightened out her dress that fit like a charm, serving up just enough sexy while still looking sophisticated. "Wow. That carpet is nuts!"

I shrugged. "They only go nuts when it's someone worth going nuts over. I told you that dress was a game-changer."

She looked down like she was second-guessing the choice.

"I mean that in a good way, Kennedy. You look... *mouthwatering* fine. You look *risk-it-all* fine. You look *rip that dress off and go in* fine. You look..."

She cut me off. "I get it, Bryson. But thank you. For rescuing me."

I closed my fists, putting them to my waist like a superhero. "Captain Save-A-Ho, at your service."

62

"Excuse me!"

Her tone was giving attitude, but there was a hint of a smile to her face as if she actually took the joke.

"I'm playin', Kenn. You're not a ho. You're *Mrs. Montgomery*," I said teasingly.

She wasted no time correcting me, "*Future* Mrs. Montgomery. I'm still *Ms.* Wilson for now."

I grabbed her hands again, feeling desperate with need to touch her in some way as I told her, "Well *Ms. Wilson* is looking scrumptious tonight. And I'm glad she decided to join me."

Kennedy

I'm not built for this.

I suppose it was partially my fault for assuming that we'd be going straight to the movie premiere and coming right back to the hotel when it was over. But no amount of practice walking around the house to mold this particular pair of heels had prepared me for being in them the whole night. My feet were on fire as I took short, calculated steps behind Bryson to the car that was supposed to be taking us to yet another after party.

I mean, what devil even came up with the concept of an after *after* party?

I'll tell you; someone with too much time on their hands.

I must've been wearing the pain on my face as the second we got in the car, Bryson felt the need to ask, "Kennedy, you good?"

I kicked off my shoes, straining to reach my feet in my too-tight dress with the limited space of the backseat as I said, "I'm fine."

"Here. Let me see."

I peeked up and he nodded towards my feet to confirm what he was talking about. But there was no way I could let him rub my feet. Then again, what kind of woman would I be to turn down a foot massage from an *obviously* strong man?

An engaged one; that's what kind.

"I'm good, Bryson. I can do it."

In all honesty, it hurt to say that out loud as my feet

continued to throb so much I was worried they'd never be able to fit back into my shoes.

"Quit being a hard ass, Kennedy. Let me do it. I went to school for reflexology."

"*You did?*"

He laughed as he said, "No. But I've had enough treatments after my games to know exactly what to do. Just trust me."

I thought it over, looking down at my feet that were visibly pulsating.

One little foot massage isn't gonna hurt anybody.

I swung my legs up to his lap in the backseat, leaning against the door for support. He smiled, looking down at my feet in a way that suddenly made me feel self-conscious about them. He grabbed one, pulling it closer to his torso before he began massaging it, hitting points that I didn't even know existed until he applied the perfect amount of pressure.

"You have some pretty feet, Kenn. Perfect, really. Not too big. No bunions. Perfectly aligned. Perfectly pedicured…" His voice began to fade in my head as I focused on his hands. My eyes seemed to close on their own as he switched to the other foot.

"Does Landon take good care of your feet? I mean, does he, you know… use them for their power?"

I answered the question in my head instead of out loud knowing Landon wasn't *at all* a feet guy.

"If you press right here, you can…"

Oh my God.

I slid further down the door as I melted in response to the pressure. It almost felt like the sensation wasn't coming from my feet at all; like my feet were just the vice used to feel pleasure somewhere else.

"And if I press this, you'll probably…"

I shuddered, using my last bit of strength and dignity

to pull my feet away.

"What the hell, Bryson?! What did you do to my feet?!" I had to look at them up close to make sure they were still normal.

He laughed, licking his lips as he innocently replied, "I didn't do anything your man shouldn't already be doing. A *real* man knows how to work his woman's feet."

Since Landon wasn't here to stand up for himself, it was up to me to stand up for him. "Landon is a real man. How else do you think he got me?"

He scooted closer to me, taking up every centimeter of personal space I had to say, "He didn't *get* you. You settled."

I turned to him, my head against the window to create some space as I defended myself. "What?! That is *so* not true."

He got even closer, his face a few mere inches away from mine. He was so close that I held my breath, not even wanting to give him the satisfaction of my release touching his lips.

"Tell yourself anything, Kennedy. But I hear you... even when you don't think I do."

This was a mistake.

I knew it.

He knew it.

Yet, he didn't care because while he was the orchestrator of his personal masterpiece, it was *my* personal disaster.

We didn't share many words after the incident in the backseat, me doing my thing and him doing his own as we mixed and mingled at the after *after* party. By the time we got back to the suite, we only had a few hours to take a quick nap before it was time to head to the airport.

I waited in the living room with my luggage as Bryson struggled to pack his own things like he had never done it before. I heard him give up on it more than a few times, threatening to leave it all there in the hotel and just buy new stuff instead of dealing with it.

What a waste.

I dropped my purse on the couch before I went in to help him, immediately seeing the problem.

"Bryson, these clothes are way too expensive for you to just... *stuff* them in a suitcase. Take them out and fold them up right."

He brushed me off, still trying to zip it up as he said, "Hell no, I'm not taking them out. I almost got it, Kennedy."

I watched a shirt I had handpicked get snagged on the zipper and knew my action had to be more urgent. "Bryson! Take. Them. Out."

Apparently, all it took was me getting stern with him for him to get the point. He stopped, unzipping the suitcase and dumping all of his clothes and shoes on the bed.

"Now fold them up nicely."

He huffed and puffed like he didn't want to do it, but I gave him the look to let him know I wasn't playing. Thankfully he went with it.

"This shit takes way too long."

"Bryson, it takes all of three minutes tops. You'll survive."

He rolled his eyes and I had to smile at the fact that *I* had the power this time around.

Once he got all of his clothes and shoes in neatly, he tried to zip it again, but it wouldn't close. "See, Kenn? Did all that shit for nothin'."

———

I walked over to the bed, giving the zipper a tug and quickly discovering it was, indeed, still jammed. I pulled it backwards before attempting to zip it again with a little more of a head start.

That didn't work either.

"Here. I'll push it shut and you zip it."

Considering the clock was ticking on how much time we had left before we absolutely had to board our plane, I really wasn't in a position to turn down the idea. But when Bryson somehow ended up directly behind me, his arms on each side of my body as he held the suitcase down, I knew it was a bad one.

I zipped the suitcase as fast as I could, giving it just enough umph for it to close. And even though the suitcase was shut, Bryson didn't move away; instead leaning in to whisper, *"Thank you, Kennedy"* in my ear.

It took a few short breaths before I could answer, "You're welcome."

I expected him to move away but he didn't, taking advantage of our closeness to nibble on my ear. The moan escaped my lips before I could catch it.

Kennedy!

I immediately snapped out of it, mustering up enough energy to push him away.

"Bryson, this has got to stop."

I tried to get even further away, but he caught me by the wrist, pulling me flush against his perfectly-crafted frame. "Why, Kennedy? Why does it have to stop? Give me one good reason why I should push away every urge of attraction I feel for you, every need I feel to touch you, every…"

I cut him off. "I am *engaged*. Not dating. Not cohabiting. *Engaged*."

"Okay. Two good reasons."

I put my hands against his chest - *always a mistake* –

———

as I reminded him, "I'm your employee."

"*Three?*"

Now I had to push him away. "Bryson! No more. Got it?"

He had the nerve to get an attitude, snatching his suitcase off the bed as he said, "You're acting like I have control of the shit. If I did, it would be easy. If I did, *of course* I wouldn't touch you. That's flat out..."

"Pathetic. Is that the word you were looking for? Pathetic?"

"No. Pathetic is you settling for someone like Landon when you *deserve* someone like me."

He's gonna get enough of talking about my man...

"Landon is my soul mate. He's righted my wrong more times than I can count. And guess what? He even lays the pipe well."

I don't know why I felt it was necessary to drop the last fact, but sex always seemed like the ultimate one-up when it came to competitions between men.

I was surprised when Bryson smirked as he said, "Well and *outstanding* are two different things. I'd like to think I'm the latter."

That stopped me dead in my tracks, forcing me to turn his way. "What fool told you your arrogance was attractive?"

He flashed me that brilliant smile as he answered, "You."

Before I could reply, there was a knock on the door signaling our car had arrived. I grabbed my suitcase and Bryson followed me with his own.

"We're not done here, Kennedy."

I didn't bother giving him my eyes, instead focusing on the door as I corrected him, "We are."

"We aren't."

I pulled the door open, dragging my suitcase close

—

70

behind. "Well I am."

He used his free hand to grab me by my wrist, turning me around in the middle of the hallway and bringing his face right in front of mine to say, "Well I'm not."

His lips were on mine before I could stop him. And I hated that I didn't really want to stop him. But this couldn't happen. Bryson kissing me so deep, his tongue knowing my every move, couldn't happen. So I pulled back, looking around to make sure no one saw us.

He wiped his lips, his cocky little grin surfacing as he said, "Now I'm done."

Bryson

"You didn't..."

My eyes remained on my lap, my head covered with a hood as I shamefully admitted, "I did."

"Bryson..."

Nothing in the world felt as bad as a legitimately disappointed Leslie. I could make her mad, piss her off to the furthest extent. *But her disappointment?*

I always had trouble swallowing that shit.

I don't know what I expected her to say when I told her that I had summoned Kennedy to the LA trip *and* kissed her, but I knew she wouldn't be thrilled with the news.

"I know, Leslie. It was stupid, but I couldn't help it. Everything about the moment felt so..."

She cut me off. "Wrong, Bryson! It should've felt wrong."

"*Should've*, but it didn't. So I guess I acted before the wrongness could surface." And boy did that shit hit me like a train the second we got in the car to leave the hotel.

She wouldn't even sit by me on the plane; had asked the gate attendant to switch her seat and volunteered to pay extra if necessary. And even when we reunited, she was completely quiet up until the time I dropped her off at her apartment when she offered me a halfhearted goodbye.

"Bryson, I gave you one job; to not ruin her. And now not only are you getting yourself involved with an employee, you're toying with her feelings."

"*Toying with her feelings?* This isn't a game, Leslie."

I tried not to be offended until she said, "That's what you always say until the next PYT strolls by and steals your attention. Then you leave the has-been desperate for her fix of you, *doing crazy shit* for her fix of you."

Though there were more than a couple crazies that came to mind, I knew that wasn't always the case. But instead of going back and forth, I decided to cut that part of the conversation short. "Okay, you got your scolding out. Now I need some advice on what to do next."

She sighed into her hands, almost as exasperated as me about the situation. "*What to do next?* What do you mean, *what to do next?* There is no *next*, Bryson. This has gotta stop before it goes too far."

"It's already gone too far! I just... I don't know what to do."

She spoke like the answer was obvious. "You don't do anything other than step away and act like none of this ever happened so we don't lose another good stylist."

"Not that easy, Leslie."

"Oh, but it is. And even if it's not, you're Bryson Harris. You can make it that easy."

I tried to digest her advice; apply it some way, somehow. But there was hardly any use.

I was in way deeper than I could handle.

"Here. There's enough outfit choices to get you through the week as long as your schedule doesn't change."

I looked at the various ensembles, each matched with shoes, that Kennedy had laid out on the couch in order of appearance. When she showed up to my house, she didn't say much; just went right to work pulling stuff from my closet. I had to be at the arena in less than an hour to prepare for my game later that night, but not even that felt more important than spending time with Kennedy talking about clothes.

"Looks good. Thank you."

She pulled her hair behind her ear, only offering a smile for a response.

I watched as she gathered her things preparing to go on about her day, but something made me stop her with my incessant staring that always seemed to make her uncomfortable.

"What is it, Bryson?"

"I wanted to tell you that... I'm sorry." After everything that had gone down, it felt like the right thing to say in the moment.

She seemed surprised as she asked, "Sorry for what?"

"Sorry for... I don't know; putting you in such a compromising position I guess."

She crossed her arms over her chest, looking at me suspiciously as she asked, "Compromising, huh? That's what you call it? *Compromising*?

I didn't see the issue, so I said, "Yeah, compromising. It was wrong for me to push up on you like that knowing you're engaged. So I'm sorry."

She stared at me for a long moment, her eyes zeroing in on mine before she spewed, "Bullshit, Bryson."

"What?"

"That's bullshit. You knew exactly what you were doing and you're hardly sorry about it. If you were really sorry, it wouldn't have taken you so many times to figure that out. If you were sorry, you wouldn't have dissed Landon over and over again. If you were sorry, *you*

---

wouldn't have… you wouldn't have kissed me."

Something about her words opened a whole new can of worms that I hardly expected to show up. I stood up, going toe-to-toe with her as I said, "You wanna talk about bullshit? Let's do it. Let's talk about this bullshit of you kissing me back. This bullshit of you moaning when I made a move. This bullshit of you tryna use Landon as the only excuse for why we can't go all the way."

She acted all disgusted as she tossed back, *"Go all the way?* Nobody wants to have sex with you, Bryson!"

"Prove it."

I pulled my shirt over my head, tossing it to the ground at her feet. She looked down at it, crossing her arms over her chest as she said, "You're pathetic."

"Pathetic, huh? All of this… is pathetic?"

I watched her chest heave up and down as she nodded her head yes. I closed the little bit of space between us so that I could speak directly into her ear. "Or is it pathetic that you want it? You want it so bad that you spend half of the time in my presence squeezing your thighs together to fight off the temptation."

She shook her head, her ear grazing my lips as she said, "That's not true."

My hands found what felt like their rightful place on her ass as I pulled her in tighter. "It is."

She didn't remove them, just let out a weak, "Bryson, stop."

"No."

"Bryson…"

I released her ass so I could grab her chin and lift it in a way that her eyes were forced to face mine. "Tell me, Kennedy. Tell me you don't want me. Tell me you're unaffected. Tell me you're so in love with Landon, so devoted to Landon."

She closed her eyes as she let out another weak plea.

"Bryson, please…"

"Tell me!"

She yanked away, getting as far away from me as she could before she admitted, "Okay! Fine! I want you, Bryson. I want you so damn bad, but I can't have you because I *do* love Landon. I *am* devoted to Landon."

"Forget, Landon!"

She fell into the couch, putting her elbows on her thighs as posts so that she could rest her face in her hands. Her speech was muffled as she said, "It doesn't work like that. Don't you get it?"

"Actually I don't."

I mean, who *wanted* someone just to stay with somebody else? It's not like the shit was forced or arranged. Kennedy had a choice.

She attempted to break it down, but I still didn't get her logic when she said, "This isn't about pleasure. Hell, this is hardly about love. It's about loyalty."

"So you're willing to compromise your happiness for loyalty?" Of all of the concepts of the day, that one certainly sounded the most bullshittiest of all.

"That's none of your business."

"Whatever, Kennedy. Deny yourself if you want to. I'm through dealing with it."

Kennedy

I have to quit.

There was no way I could keep working with Bryson after all that had went down over the last couple of days.

We got too heated, too fast.

We said too much

We... we kissed.

And it felt so damn good.

Scary good.

So scary that I knew I had to stay as far away from him as possible.

I gave things a test drive by trying to do my job as normal, but even that turned into an *almost, too close* situation. One second I was calling him out, the next second he had handfuls of my ass. Big handfuls as if I really had that much to give. But somehow it was a perfect fit for his greedy palms.

I looked at the clock on the nightstand, and though it was well before I was supposed to report for duty, there was no way I could get another wink of sleep. I slipped out of bed, trying not to wake Landon as I made my way to the living room. I turned on the TV, and of course, who was the first one plastered on the screen?

Bryson Harris.

A triple-double. How convenient.

While he was moving on with his life, handling business as usual, I was stuck tight-roping the fine line between business and pleasure. But if he could keep business as business, why couldn't I do the same?

Because he's fine as hell, and his lips taste like sin, and he smells good, and....

"Kennedy, what are you doing up so early?"

I jumped from my spot on the couch, finding a shirtless Landon who was busy scrubbing his eyes.

"Umm, I... couldn't sleep." I left it at that, knowing I would probably talk myself into a corner if I said anymore.

He looked at me suspiciously, his eyes still squinty as they tried to adjust to the light. "You alright, babe?"

The last thing I needed was for him to worry, so I answered, "*Yeah.* Yeah, I'm fine. I think I'm gonna... go for a jog or something."

Because that's what people do in these type of needing-to-clear-my-head situations, right?

He immediately started to laugh. "Kennedy, you haven't worked out since I've been with you. Do you even own a pair of running shoes?"

"Do sneaker wedges count?"

He laughed even harder.

"Babe, you'll bust your head wide open trying to run in those things. Here, how about we skip the jog and try another... cardio activity?"

"Like what?"

He walked over to where I sat on the couch, dropping to his knees right in front of me. Then he parted my thighs, causing the oversized t-shirt I fell asleep in to ride up. His sly grin told me exactly what he was up to and I certainly wasn't going to stop him if *this* was the alternative to running all of the two blocks I could survive.

A little morning sex would be the perfect thing to get my mind off of Bryson.

—

80

I was humming - *literally humming* - as I rang the doorbell at Bryson's house. Spending the morning all over the apartment with Landon was the perfect reminder of why I was planning on marrying him.

He was good to me.

He *felt* good to me.

And though he may not always make my heart race or cause me to fumble over my words and lose my breath with his mere presence, he loved me and cared for me in a way that no other man had shown me before.

Bryson would never measure up to that.

So when he opened the door all shirtless and sexy, I didn't even flinch. I faced him straight up, telling him good morning before I proceeded right past him into his home like I owned the place. I waited for him to close the door and follow me, but instead he stayed in the doorway just looking at me.

"Aren't you gonna say good morning back?"

His face was tense as he replied, "No. I'm too busy trying to figure out what the hell got into you."

I really wanted to answer, *"My man got into me. All over the place. All morning long."* But that wouldn't have exactly been professional, so I said, "I'm just in a good mood. That's all."

He closed the door, but still didn't look convinced. "Nah, I've seen your good moods. And you haven't exactly been a good mood person lately, so this is different."

I brushed him off. "Whatever, Bryson. Can we just get to the closet so I can do my job and get out of here?"

He finally smiled, his bicep flexing as he brought his hand to his chin to stroke it. "Actually, I have a special assignment for you. I need you to come to this photo-shoot with me."

I caught an attitude quick. "What? Why? Don't they have a stylist of their own?"

He could tell I was flustered so he took a step closer to me, his voice dropping an octave as he said, "But I want *my* stylist there."

I held his eyes for a moment, refusing to back down from the challenge of his presence.

I could do this.

I could face Bryson straight up without falling into his traps.

I could... *damn, that smile.*

In what seemed like slow motion, Bryson brought his hand to my face, stroking my cheek as he said, "You look beautiful today, Kennedy. Glowing in fact. Like you got some."

I snatched my face away, heading to his state-of-the-art kitchen to grab a bottle of water. And of course he was right on my heels, each of his barefooted steps matching the clank of my chunky heeled ankle booties against his hardwood floor.

"My sex life is none of your business, *boss*," I tossed over my shoulder as I yanked the refrigerator door open.

The second I bent over to grab a bottle from the bottom shelf, I felt Bryson directly behind me, his hands on my waist and his pelvis right against my ass. I closed my eyes, immediately picking up on the fact that he couldn't have possibly had on any boxers... *or briefs*. But no matter how good he felt, I had to handle this the right way.

I had to be strong.

So I stood up - *not panicked, or urgently* - but just enough so that our bodies could separate. Then I closed the door and turned around right into his usual cocky

—

expression to ask, "Where's the photo-shoot?"

He looked even more confused than I expected. "*The photo-shoot*? That's what you wanna talk about? *The photo-shoot*?"

"That's why I'm here, isn't it? To do my job? The job you hired me to do?"

He was at a loss, rubbing a hand against the nape of his neck and letting out a spacey, "Yeah... yeah, I... I guess so."

"Good. Now let's get to work."

Bryson

Kennedy had been floating between the dressing room and set all afternoon. And though it should've made me happy to see her happy, it didn't because I knew I had nothing to do with it. In fact, she was beyond pissed the last time she left my house, so her newfound excitement about life had to be a result of wack ass Landon. She didn't talk about their relationship much other than surface-level shit like how much she loved him, but I was interested to see exactly what type of dude he was.

I smiled through the last set of fifty frames before the shoot was finally called to a close. Then I headed to the dressing room where I figured Kennedy was hiding out for a break. I opened the door and found her leaning on the arm of the couch fast asleep. She looked radiant, her makeup and hair for the day still completely intact as she let out short puffs of breath.

I felt like I could watch her do this all day, but I didn't want to creep her out in the event that she actually woke up. So instead, I sat down next to her, pushing her hair over her shoulder before tapping her awake.

Her eyes flashed open for a second, but quickly closed again as she readjusted in her seat on the couch.

"Kennedy. Kennedy, wake up."

"Five more minutes," she pleaded.

I wanted to give her all the time in the world, but I knew she didn't really mean it. So I tapped her shoulder once more. "Kennedy, you can sleep in the car. We gotta go. I have a flight to catch."

The mention of a flight woke her right up.

"Oh my God! I can't believe I... how long was I..." She rushed over to the mirror, checking her face and rearranging her hair.

I stood up, finding a spot right behind her in the mirror as I told her, "Relax, Kennedy. We're all done with the shoot and you were only out for ten minutes tops."

Her hands fell to the countertop as she put her head down, trying to pull herself together. Then she turned around, facing me with the most embarrassed expression. "I'm so sorry. I just... didn't get much sleep last night."

The smirk came on its own as I reminded her, "We figured that out earlier, remember?"

She rolled her eyes as she made her way past me, snatching her purse off the couch before she headed out of the door.

Something about her was different.

She was edgier, feistier, even more intriguing.

I was in big trouble.

"Shit, Bryson! Right there!"

I drove into Nicole as hard as I could, desperate for a release. After spending time with Kennedy - *touching Kennedy* -, I knew the only way I could fight the urge to have her was to take it out on somebody else. This time, it just so happened to be a lucky groupie after my away game. I didn't indulge in groupies *that* often, but something about the butter-pecan chick in the hella tight dress got me to change my mind for the night.

Nicole had already gotten hers twice, so I figured it was fair for me to get my own. I went a little harder, hitting all the right spots and causing her to let out porno-worthy screams even though I was doing it for my own selfish reasons. The selfish reasons that had me grunting before I released every ounce of build-up into the condom.

Nicole blushed as she rolled over to her back, pulling the cover up and over her naked body. She was biting her bottom lip, holding back a major grin like she was embarrassed by something. And just when I was getting ready to ask her about it, she said, "I've never done this before."

I panicked, hoping I hadn't done something crazy like taken the poor girl's virginity.

"You've never done what?" I asked cautiously.

"Had sex on the first night."

Whew.

That still surprised me considering it didn't take much for me to convince her to do so. But she actually seemed like a nice girl, one who I wouldn't have a problem doubling back on later if I was ever in her city again.

I hopped out of bed to go clean myself up in the bathroom as I yelled behind me, "Well I hope I made it worth your while."

Her answer was low, but I still heard her clearly as she replied, "That and more, Bryson. That and more."

Kennedy

I felt pitiful as I sat in my apartment alone watching Bryson's postgame interview on what had to be its third loop on *SportsCenter*. Landon was at the club again, so it was just me, my carton of *Talenti*, and my bottle of wine until either he made it back or I fell asleep; though I didn't see sleep coming anytime soon.

No matter how hard of a front I was able to put up in Bryson's presence, that didn't stop my real feelings from surfacing when I was alone. Like now, when I wanted nothing more than to be wrapped in a pair of strong arms as I dozed off to a movie while snuggled up on the couch.

Landon's arms are pretty strong, Kennedy.

My eyes were locked on the TV as I stared at Bryson's arms that were squeezing against the sleeves of his blazer, the blazer that I had picked out for him. In fact, Bryson looked good in just about everything I dressed him in which made my job slightly easier.

Landon dresses well too, Kennedy.

I continued watching the interview and comparing the two, though I knew there was really no comparison. While Bryson was all hot, and sexy, and thrill, Landon was sweet. Landon was comfortable. Landon was home.

There wasn't a decision for me to make.

It was already made the second I said, "Yes".

I turned the TV off, pouring the last of the wine into my glass before taking it and the couple bites of *Talenti* I had left with me to the bedroom. I almost left my phone until it began buzzing against the coffee table. I doubled back, taking a peek at the screen and immediately rolling my eyes at the message.

My flight gets in at 9. I'll need you to come by around 10 to fit me for the game. - B$

I thought about ignoring it, pretending like I had already fallen asleep when it came. But I had to remind myself that he was my boss.

Kennedy: I'll be there.

Miss you, Kenn. Can't wait to see you in the morning. ;) - B$

I chugged my wine, not even saving a sip to savor. I mean, what was I supposed to say to that?

How could I logically reply to something so simple yet so... *ugh*.

Bryson knew exactly what he was doing, knew exactly how to get under my skin, and had to know I'd be vulnerable on a night like tonight when I was just slightly past the point of tipsy. I typed and deleted a bunch of stupid responses before I came up with one that I could live with in the morning.

Kennedy: See you then, boss.

"You and your man should come to the game tonight."

Bryson spoke of the idea so casually as if it was even possible that I'd subject myself to such torture. It was already plenty for me to be looking at his forever shirtless frame as he packed his duffle bag. The last thing I needed to be doing was seeing him all sweaty in live action.

"We can't. We already have plans," I lied as I diverted my eyes elsewhere.

He stopped, peeking up at me with a smile as he said, "No plans are bigger than courtside seats."

—

Courtside? "Matter of fact, why don't you call your man right now and tell him the news."

I thought it over, knowing Landon would probably kill me for turning down the tickets. But I had to stay strong.

"Our plans are pretty important."

Non-existently important.

He eyed me again before he walked over to where I was standing and snatched my phone from my hand. I didn't budge, knowing he wouldn't be able to access anything without... "What's your passcode?"

I crossed my arms over my chest as I protested, "I'm not telling you."

He stepped closer, his bare, tattooed chest only a few inches from mine as he asked, "Kennedy, do you want me to tickle it out of you? Kiss it out of you? Lick it out of..."

I put my hand up to stop him. "Fine! It's 0315."

He laughed in victory, typing it in and surely scrolling to my call log. "What is that anyway? The day ol' boy proposed to you?"

It was a shame that I didn't even remember *that* exact date, but I quickly answered him. "No. It's my birthday."

He stopped scrolling the second he realized what I had said. "Wait a minute. 0315. March 15th. That's today! Kennedy, it's your birthday and you didn't tell anybody?"

I brushed him off, knowing it wasn't as big of a deal as he was making it. "Who tells people it's their birthday? Like... you really thought I was just gonna come in here and announce something like that? That'd be weird."

He still didn't look satisfied as he asked, "How old are you?"

91

"Twenty… *five*." I cringed saying it out loud.

Surely I was engaged, had a great job with benefits, a decent place to lay my head at night, and a savings account; but I hardly felt like I had my shit together enough to already be hitting this particular milestone.

To make matters even worse, Bryson replied, "I thought you were older than that."

I couldn't help but to be offended. "What?! Why?"

He only shrugged, going back to his packing as he said, "I don't know. You're just so… mature. Responsible. Uptight."

My attitude remained. "*Uptight*? I am *not* uptight."

He disappeared into the closet, grabbing a pair of tennis shoes before he spoke again. "Kennedy, let's be real here. You're not exactly a thrill seeker. You play it safe. You calculate your moves. You're thorough. And there's nothing wrong with that. It's just not very… twenty-fiveish."

I crossed my arms over my chest, feeling the need to defend my morals. "It is when you're not making millions. Not all of us can throw our lives away at the expense of fast cars and faster women."

Now he was the offended one, biting the inside of his cheek before he piped out, "That's what you think I do?"

I challenged him, "That's what I know you do."

He took a few steps closer to me as he asked, "What about my charities? Annual events in the community? Community service partnerships?"

I brushed off the name dropping. "For every *one* of those, there's probably *three* whores you've left in each city you've visited. I know your type, Bryson. I'm no fool."

He knew I was right, but I was surprised when he responded, "Kennedy, I'm young. I'm single. Of course I indulge. But what's your excuse?"

"*My excuse*? My excuse for what?"

He covered the little space left between us, getting right in my face to ask, "Your excuse for being twenty-five, and responsible, but still wanting to risk it all for a chance with *irresponsible, reckless ass* me?"

I refused to back down. "What are you talking about, Bryson?"

His hands were around my waist before I could move away. "Kennedy, I'm being real with you. So keep that in mind when I tell you we might as well get this over with so we can resume our normal lives."

I still didn't move. "Get what over with?"

"This... exploration. *Sexually*. Me and you. And don't say you're not curious cause it's been written all over your face for a while now."

Now I had to pull away.

"My God. You can't possibly be this full of yourself all the time."

He smirked, finding my wrist to pull me back but not completely as he said, "Not all the time. Just long enough to get the attention of pretty women like yourself."

Since he liked to get in my face to prove his point, I stood on my tippy-toes to do the same. "I don't wanna have sex with you, Bryson. So just let it go, alright?"

Somehow his hands ended up back on my waist like he just owned the damn place.

His voice was low and gentle as he teased, "You don't, huh? You sure about that?"

My feet fell flat as I answered, "*I'm...* I'm positive."

Don't you start fumbling over your words now, Kennedy!

He eyed me, licking his lips in a way he just knew would send my lower half into a frenzy. "Well why are you breathing all funny, huh? Can't stand for me to be

—

93

this close? Can't stand for me to… tease you?"

I tipped my head back to meet his eyes. "Bryson, I don't want you."

His face quickly hovered over mine, our lips so close that if I were to get on my tippy-toes again we'd definitely be kissing. "You're lying. You already told me you wanted me. And I want you too. So let me have you, Kennedy. Let me…"

My phone began to ring in Bryson's pocket, cutting him off. He didn't step away, just pulled it out and pressed the green button to answer it before putting it to my ear so that I could catch it against my shoulder.

"Hey birthday girl. What are you up to?"

I was just getting ready to answer Landon's question when Bryson dropped to his knees in front of me, sliding the edge of my dress up against my tights. "I'm at… I'm at work, babe. What's up?" I tried to shoo Bryson away, but he locked both of my hands with one of his as he continued to push my dress up with the other.

"Nothing much, just making sure you're having a good day. We gonna do dinner tonight? Maybe a movie? I mean, it's totally up to you since it's your day and all."

I was trying to pay attention, but Bryson stuck his face right in the crotch of my leggings causing me to yelp, "Yes! I mean… *actually*, Bryson gave me… gave *us* courtside tickets to the game. For my birthday." I looked down at Bryson with wide eyes and he only smirked as he tugged on my leggings that I knew he wouldn't be able to pull off with one hand.

"What?! You're kidding me! That's dope, Kennedy! So what time should I meet you at home?"

I felt a rush of cold air against my thighs, looking back down to find that Bryson had, indeed, figured it out.

How the hell did he…?

"Six! I mean… how's six o' clock sound?"

—

94

God, please forgive me.

"I should be able to make it by then. Well I'm excited. Make sure you're extra nice to Bryson today for that sweet gift," he said with a laugh that just about made me explode. Well, it was either that or the fact that Bryson's lips were grazing my inner thigh in a way that had me struggling not to moan.

"I... I will. See you at six."

I waited until I heard him end the call since I couldn't do it myself. Then I dropped the phone so that it would land right on Bryson's head.

He let my hands go as he yelled, "Ouch! What the fuck, Kenn?!"

I stepped away, pulling my leggings up as quickly as I could before sliding my dress back down. "What the fuck *you*, Bryson?! I was on the phone with my damn fiancé and you were getting ready to..." I couldn't even say it out loud.

"Well Kennedy. I'm afraid to break it to you, but uhh... I'm not the only bad guy here." Then he stood up, heading back to his closet as he casually tossed out, "The tickets will be at Will Call."

Bryson

The game was over and won with hardly any help of mine. Anytime there was a break in game action, my eyes were on Kennedy and her fiancé as they shared drinks, fed each other popcorn, wiped excess food off of each other's faces and did all that other cute shit only couples could do.

I suppose it was my fault for extending the tickets in the first place. But now that I had gotten a sample of Kennedy - even if it was just a kiss against her thigh and a whiff of her sweet womanly scent - I was craving a full dose. And when I looked Landon in his eyes and shook his hand, I already felt guilty about the fact that I was *definitely* going to fulfill that craving.

"It's so good to meet you, man. I've been following your career since your college days at the University of California."

"Oh really? That's what's up. It's always cool to meet a *loyal* fan." My eyes went to Kennedy just as she put her head down. "So, what do you two have planned for the rest of the evening?" Knowing Kennedy, she'd probably be going home to knit a sweater or some shit.

Landon smirked, damn near blushing as he said, "We're actually getting ready to... Kennedy, why don't you tell him?"

Kennedy rolled her eyes as she announced with zero enthusiasm, "We're going to the strip club. So my boring twenty-five-year-old ass can throw some one's on some not-so-boring ass. For my birthday."

My eyebrow shot up on its own.

Kennedy?

At a strip club?

Now that I'd have to see to believe. I mean, I had seen her at the regular club once before, but she hardly seemed to be enjoying it then.

"I'd love to join you guys. If you don't mind."

Landon lit up like a kid on Christmas. "You serious?! Hell yeah you can join us! My uncle is the owner and he's a huge Philly fan, so I know for a fact he'll give you nothing but the best."

I looked over to Kennedy for approval, and of course she refused to give me her eyes. But her little attitude wasn't enough to stop me from coming.

So I gave Landon a smile as I told him, "Sounds good, bro. I'll meet y'all there."

I arrived at the strip club way later than I anticipated. I could only hope that Kennedy and Landon were still there, but I wouldn't be surprised if Kennedy had already called it a night.

Instead of coming through the front door and causing a scene, I had one of my teammates, Wes, coordinate our entrance through the back. I wasn't inside the building for more than a minute before I saw Landon waving us over. "Bryson! Wes! Over here."

Since Wes hadn't met Landon, he looked back at me with a confused expression. But I gave him the nod to let him know it was cool. We headed his way, but my eyes were scanning the crowd as I tried to find Kennedy.

I know her ass didn't really go home already...

"Yo, I didn't know you were bringing guests too! What's up, Wes?"

—

Wes looked Landon up and down before asking him, "And you are..."

I could tell he was a little embarrassed, so I answered for him, "This is Landon. His girl works for me."

Wes instantly busted out laughing. "Bruh, you trust this man working with your woman?! Do you know who he is?!"

Landon let out a laugh of his own as he replied, "I don't have to trust him. I trust Kennedy. She would never betray me; especially for a guy like this dude." *Little do you know...* "There she goes now."

I followed his gaze to the door and my jaw hit the ground once I laid eyes on her. Kennedy was looking like... *fuck.* Hardly like the Kennedy I had become familiar with. Even though it was still pretty cold outside, she was showing as much skin as legally allowed; her boobs refusing to be contained by the thin lace fabric of her white crop top. She complemented it with a white mini skirt that squeezed her thighs and ass in all the right places. Even Wes was impressed as he let out a low, *"Damn."*

I looked behind her and saw she had arrived with a friend, the same one from before. But before I could even think to address her, she brushed past me and went straight to Landon, falling into his arms for a hug.

"There's my birthday girl. You good, babe?"

She served him a flirty smile as she nodded her head yes.

I could tell something was off about her, but I couldn't put my finger on it right away until her friend announced, "Landon, I told her to drink some water, but she refused."

Ahh that's what it is.
Kennedy's already drunk.

———

This ought to be good.

Kennedy shrugged them both off as she shouted, "It's my birthday! Drinking water kinda defeats the point."

Landon looked like he wanted to say something, but quickly decided to keep his thoughts to himself.

"Happy Birthday, Kennedy. I don't know if you remember me, but I'm Wes." He stuck his hand out and she gave him the same flirty smile that she gave Landon as she returned the gesture.

Damn, she's really on one.

Her voice was syrupy sweet as she told him, "Thank you, Wes. And thanks for coming to celebrate with me."

He still hadn't let her hand go, giving it a little kiss before he replied, "Don't thank me. Thank Bryson for dragging me out with him."

Her eyes went to mine, her smile never faltering as she said in a low, sexy tone, "Thank you, Bryson."

I could hardly speak looking at her dressed like this, and smelling like this, and... *shit.*

This was a bad idea.

Kennedy

The music was too loud.

My head was too hazy.

I couldn't... I couldn't even think straight, so I knew I had gone too far.

Everyone around me was having a good time, including Landon who at first glance looked just as drunk as I was while he talked to his Uncle and Wes. Bryson, on the other hand, had his eyes fixated on the stage as a girl I knew as Brandy glided her way down the pole under the name Sapphire.

Brandy was definitely one of the more athletic strippers, climbing all nine feet of the pole before cascading down using only her thighs to hang on with. Bryson stood up and headed to the stage, throwing a stack of ones in the air to land on her. She smiled before she headed his way, bending over right in front of him to give him a personal show for his contribution. And I felt...

"Kennedy, it's almost time for your birthday dance!" Chloe's voice cut my daze short.

But then I realized what she had said and asked, "Birthday dance?"

"Yes, girl! And you're the only birthday girl in the building so you'll get to keep all the money!" I could tell her excitement was solely for that fact as if she was going to get a cut of it.

I took a quick sip from the birthday flask she had gifted me before I told her, "Chloe, I am *not* getting on that stage."

Sure I was drunk, but I wasn't *that* damn drunk.

"You have to, Kennedy! It's your birthday, you're already here, and it's not like you have to take your clothes off. Just stand up there and shake ya ass a little bit, use the pole if you want to; live a little!"

Something about that final statement struck me.

Live a little.

Would it really be that bad to let my hair down a little more than it already was tonight?

Like she said, it *was* my birthday and I *was* here to have fun. And my man was here, so it wasn't like I was just out here being crazy without his approval. Hell, if he could look at and enjoy the other girls, then he would certainly enjoy looking at me.

"We got a birthday girl in the house! Y'all show some love to Kennedy!"

Before I could think twice - *which was a pain to do anyway* - I headed to the stage under the watchful eye of Bryson. My eyes flashed over to Landon who looked even more impressed to see me up there. And then the song came on and something powerful came over me. It was one of my favorites, *Quickie* by Miguel, so naturally my body responded with every little sensual move I would do if I was listening to the song on my own, hypnotized by the request of a quickie over the need to be loved.

I grabbed the pole, using it to keep me stable as I grinded down to the floor, sweeping my ass against the stage before I bounced back up. Then a few dollars hit my back and I realized what I was really doing. I turned around, ready to get mad at whoever threw them until I saw who it was.

Bryson with his stupid little, sexy ass grin and a handful of ones.

I challenged him, turning back around as I strutted slowly with my hand still on the pole. I wasn't sure I'd be able to last the whole song, so I just let it take me wherever I was supposed to go. But when I closed my eyes, all I could see was me and Bryson in his massive ass house, doing this same exact thing without an audience.

In my head, I left the pole and headed right over to him with far less clothes on, locking my hands on his thighs as I grinded against his lap. His hands were all over me, sliding from my breasts to my belly button and then further. My head flew back the second he made contact and I melted with my back against his chest.

"Give it up for Kennedy, y'all!"

My eyes flew open in shock, but I quickly recovered with a smile as I watched one of the guys sweep up all the money I had apparently earned. My skin was hot and I had to pee, so I went straight from the stage to the bathroom. I knew it would probably be a mistake to break the seal, but I couldn't hold it any longer; especially with the extra pressure from me being way too turned on for my own good.

After relieving myself, I exited the stall and bumped right into Bryson.

"What the hell are you doing in here?"

He didn't answer me; just picked me up and pressed my back against the wall before he bombarded my mouth with the most urgent kiss I had ever received. I could literally feel every ounce of sexual tension we had built pouring into me and I knew right then that there was no stopping the current.

He used his free hand to push my skirt to my waist before yanking my panties to shreds. Then he dropped down in front of me, hoisting my legs over each of his shoulders and diving face first in between my thighs.

103

I almost cried the second his warm tongue brushed against my flesh. It was so swollen, so sensitive in a way that it had never been before. And Bryson was holding nothing back; licking, and sucking, and kissing me within an inch of my life.

What a way to die.

It hadn't been more than a minute before I was unleashing everything I had right into his mouth. And he embraced it, groaning as he licked every drop of my release.

When my heart rate finally calmed down, I climbed off of his shoulders; embarrassed, and ashamed, and horny all at once. I mean, the bathroom probably wasn't even locked and Landon was right outside!

Bryson looked in the mirror, cleaning himself up before he flashed me another one of those smiles. I could only watch in shock as he headed to the door, but not without tossing out, "Happy Birthday, Kennedy."

Then he left.

And *now*... now I really wanted to cry.

"Babe, you got a package."

I rolled over on the couch, my head throbbing and my throat sore as I tried to remember the events from the night before. I hardly remembered making it back to the apartment, but I knew for a fact that I deserved the couch; though I was sure Landon had no idea why I had subconsciously chosen it over being in the bed with him.

Last night had easily gone down in history as the best and worst birthday ever. And though it had thankfully ended with me safely at my apartment, I knew the chaos of it all was far from over.

I drug myself from the couch to the kitchen where

Landon had left the package on the counter. I knew I hadn't ordered anything online in ages, so I legitimately had no idea what it was.

I used scissors to break through the first cardboard box then pulled out another box that was wrapped with a bow. Attached to the bow was a note.

These would've been on time if you would've told me about your birthday. But since you like to be hardheaded, Happy Belated, Kenn.
BS
P.S. I can still taste you on my lips. ;)

I shuddered, ripping the note to shreds and tossing it in the trash before Landon could come back and see it. Then I pulled the bow from the box, opening it to find a pair of *Louboutin* pumps. In fact, they were the same exact pumps that I had pulled for Monica to wear but in my size.

What a dog.

I grabbed my phone to fire off an impulsive text that I probably should've just left as a draft but decided to send anyway.

Kennedy: So you think you can just eat me out in strip club bathrooms and buy me expensive shoes, then I'm just supposed to what? Run into your arms?

I heard the shower come on just as a reply came in.

LOL! Relax, Kenn. It was just a... heat of the moment thing. And the shoes were a gift. Enjoy them. - BS

Against every ounce of fashionista I had in my body, I fired back: **I don't want them.**

You can give them back if you want to, but the head game you'll never forget ;) - BS

Damn, he's got a point.

Landon was an incredible lover, but I'd be damned if Bryson didn't know exactly what to do with my body on the first try. Surely he'd get even better with practice, and...

I heard the shower cut off, bringing me back to reality. But more importantly, bringing forth the guilt of the conversation I would have to have with Landon. It wouldn't be fair for me to go into a marriage holding back such a massive secret.

Kennedy: I hate you.
Love you too, Kenn. ;) - BS

Bryson

"You idiot!"

I felt every inkling of remorse that Leslie wanted me to as she paced back and forth in her office. I read the papers over and over to myself knowing they couldn't be true, but that didn't make the news any less shocking.

I always used condoms and Nicole told me she was on birth control, so there was no way she could be pregnant.

At least, not by me.

"Leslie, I'm tellin' you. I didn't get that girl pregnant. Yeah we had sex, but I didn't get her pregnant. Hell, I flushed the condom myself."

It was a ritual of mine to tie it and flush it, even if it did manage to flood the toilet. It was better that than have some girl sneak it home with her in her bra or some other crazy shit like that.

Leslie finally settled down, sitting on the edge of her desk to say, "Well even if it's not yours, it's still too early to find out. She has to be at least ten weeks before we can do an actual DNA test and that's way too long as far as your reputation is concerned."

I could already see the headlines now labeling me as a deadbeat.

"Can't we just pay her to keep quiet until we know for sure?" I had no problem letting a few thousand go for the sake of my sanity.

Leslie stood up, going to her not-so-secret stash of alcohol and pouring herself a glass of scotch. "You can pay her if you want to, as long as you plan on putting in an application for a second job at the same time. She's smart, Bryson. And so are her numbers."

I was curious as to what price she named, but I believed Leslie enough to know it had to be something outrageous.

My face fell to my hands. "This is some bullshit, man."

That fired Leslie right back up, causing her to chug her scotch and biting at the burn before she stuck a scolding finger at me to say, "No. Bullshit is you out here fuckin' women you know are out to get you. A one-night stand is the easiest trick in the book, Bryson."

"I'm pretty sure I've had enough one-night stands to know that shit which is why I play it as safe as I do. She's lying."

She brushed me off, pouring herself another glass. "Whatever, Bryson. Just... keep it in your pants until we can figure this shit out."

Kennedy's eyes were surprisingly bright as she strolled into my house to do her usual task of getting my clothes together for the week. She didn't even say anything when I opened the door for her, just strutted right past me and got to work. I didn't really know what to say to her with the news from Leslie on my mind, but there was certainly no need to bring it up. Surely it would be public information before long.

She finished up, dusting her hands off before she dug in her purse and pulled out an envelope. "This is for you."

I just looked at it, having no clue what it could be. "Here. Take it."

I rubbed the back of my neck before I accepted it, pulling back the flap and removing the single page letter. After scanning the first few lines, I immediately recognized what it was.

"Wait a minute. You're resigning?"

She smiled as she answered, "That's right, Bryson. I'm resigning. I'll give you the courtesy of a two-week notice which should give you plenty of time to find a replacement. I'm sure the ladies will be beating down your door for the position, and to be real, I'm more than happy to give it away."

This was literally the last thing I needed to be happening.

I mean, what was I supposed to do without Kennedy?

She was *way* more than just my stylist.

She was my... *energy*.

I counted on the times of the day when she would come over all bubbly and innocent just to be corrupted by me; in a good way.

I tried not to sound as exhausted as I felt when I asked, "Why are you quitting on me, Kennedy?"

She shifted all of her weight to one leg, crossing her arms over her chest to answer, "You know exactly why I'm quitting, Bryson. After what you did..." she paused before correcting herself, "after what I allowed because it's not all your fault, I can't possibly continue to work for you."

"Is it because I did it or because you enjoyed it?"

"Does it matter?"

I stood up, walking over to her and uncrossing her arms so I could be even closer. "Yes, it matters. So answer the question. Is it because I did it or because you enjoyed it?"

She shrugged, rolling her eyes as she answered, "I

don't know. Maybe both? Either way, it was the final straw. I can't... do this anymore."

I took her hands as I unashamedly begged, "Kennedy, please. *You can't...* you can't leave me like this. Not right now."

She snatched her hands away as she yelled, "You're acting like I have a choice! I don't do this kinda stuff, Bryson. I'm not that girl. *I...* I love Landon. And since you can't seem to get that through your thick ass head, I have to take real action. This is where it ends."

I should've felt the words in my head, or maybe it should've gone in one ear and out the other. But something about these particular words fell right against my chest as if somebody had gotten a clean punch off without me seeing it.

But I couldn't stop.

I had to fight.

So I used the last thing I had in my arsenal. "Landon doesn't make you feel as good as I do. Landon doesn't get you all fired up the way I do. Landon doesn't..."

She cut me off. "Stop it, Bryson! Quit talking about what Landon doesn't do and think about yourself! Besides turning me on, you do *nothing* for me. *You aren't...* you aren't *shit* to me other than my boss and a headache. So just leave me alone. Let me live."

Now that was the gut punch.

I mean, what could I possibly say back to that?

She chose and it wasn't me. I'd just have to swallow my pride and accept it.

"Fine, Kennedy. Two weeks."

Kennedy

I scrolled through pages and pages of job listings, my eyes straining from looking at the computer screen for too long. In my head, I knew I'd probably never find anything even remotely as good as I had it with Bryson, but it wasn't an option to stop looking. Landon and I had gotten way too used to the extra income to take a step backwards, so I had to do everything I could to find something in the next two weeks.

Two weeks.

Two more long ass weeks with Bryson.

I wanted to cry just thinking about it.

I would miss the laid-back work environment, the laughs we shared even when he wasn't intentionally being funny, the positive vibes he always seemed to radiate even when I wasn't the most pleasant person, and *his smile…* the smile that had gotten me in trouble in the first place.

But there was no turning back now.

My resignation letter was signed, sealed, and delivered.

It was time for me to move on.

I scrolled through another page of listings, finding a job that looked at least halfway decent and submitted my information.

At least now I had something to show for myself on my resume.

I closed my laptop, completely exhausted by the process. But turning on the TV only made things worse as I somehow landed on *ESPN*. The commentators were bashing Bryson for having one of the worst games of his career. When they flashed to his postgame interview, he looked completely withdrawn, his eyes carrying an unusual shadow as if he hadn't been sleeping.

As I listened to a few of the questions, I quickly realized he was in borderline robot mode, giving the most rehearsed answers with hardly any thought. I really hated seeing him like this, especially with the possibility that I had something to do with it. But there was nothing left to say, nothing left to do, nothing to hold onto.

The game was over.

We were done.

"So! How soon can you start?"

I looked across the table at the woman I knew I could style but wasn't completely sold on. Something about her just didn't seem... *authentic*, though I couldn't put my finger on it right away. But since I'd only be with Bryson for twelve more days exactly, I knew I didn't have much of a choice when it came to accepting the position.

"My current position ends in a little under two weeks, so it would be immediately after that."

She lit up, clapping her hands together as she said, "That's perfect! I should have my settlement by then."

My interest in the woman piqued even more.

"Settlement? What kind of settlement are we talking about, Nicole?"

I knew it might have been overstepping to ask, but I couldn't help myself. And there was no way I could accept a position based on some unsure money.

She leaned a little further into the table and

whispered, "Girl, I hit the jackpot. I'm pregnant. And it's Bryson Harris's baby."

For a split second, my heart stopped beating.

I couldn't have possibly heard her right, so I asked just to make sure I wasn't trippin', "Bryson Harris? Like the basketball player?"

She smacked her lips together as she replied, "Yes, hunny. The *champion*. We had sex when he came to my city and *bam*... there's a baby."

Oh. My. God.

"And you're sure it's his?"

She brushed me off with a swat of her hand. "Does it matter? He believes it's his, so he's giving me what I want to keep it under wraps until he's ready to go public. He even moved me here to make sure I laid low."

No way!

I tried to keep my face neutral as I replied, "Wow. That's... *wow*."

There was hardly any use in trying to form a logical sentence, and it was clear she didn't care either way as she went on and on about him.

"I Googled his net worth and hunny, he's worth millions on *millions*. Can you say payday? Hell, I'll be able to pay somebody to watch this damn child for me so I can live the life I always dreamed of."

What a bitch!

I couldn't believe the girl was running the oldest scheme in the book. But even more so, I couldn't believe that Bryson was buying into it. Hell, maybe he wasn't actually down over me. He could've been down over this situation, knowing he'd be paying big for the next eighteen years of his life.

Then again, this wasn't about Bryson's doings. This was about my livelihood; my career. So instead of getting wrapped up in his drama, I told her, "You can do

———

113

whatever you want as long as my check clears."

Bryson

She wouldn't even look at me.

It was Kennedy's last week on the job and she wouldn't even give me the privilege of her eyes, knowing they were the windows to her soul. I understood her uneasiness, but it seemed like the layer was even thicker than usual. Even when I said things to deliberately get on her nerves or did things I knew would annoy her, she seemed completely unfazed; moving right along to get things done as quickly as possible.

And I couldn't stand it.

So when I caught her coming out of my closet, I cut her off so that she was forced to acknowledge me. She still didn't look at me, just tried to squeeze past me as she offered a low, "Excuse me, Bryson."

I moved in closer. "No. You're not excused. We need to talk."

Her voice remained low and her eyes stayed down as she replied, "I'm not here to talk. I'm here to do my job and go on about my day. Now if you have a problem with that, then we can surely cut this little week short. I could honestly care less about the money at this point."

I let her get past, but still followed her as she headed down the stairs.

"Well if you're not here for the money, then why are you here?"

She sighed heavily, turning around to shoot me a scowl before continuing down the stairs.

"Because I have an obligation to be here, that's

why."

I watched as she snatched her jacket and purse from the couch preparing to leave. But there was no way I was letting her get away with so much negative energy surrounding us.

I followed her to the door as I asked, "So that's what I am to you now? Not a want, or a need, but an obligation?" Of everything Kennedy had ever said to me, that one easily offended me the most.

She worked to get her jacket on and I stepped in to help her. "That's exactly what you are. The only reason I'm here is because I signed a contract."

"Oh, you mean the same contract that said *'any consensual sex between Mr. Bryson Harris and Ms. Kennedy Wilson may be deemed grounds for immediate termination unless specified beforehand'*?"

Her tone reeked of sarcasm as she replied, "Terminate me. *Please*. I'm begging you."

I opened the door for her, but not without saying, "You and I both know that'd be way too easy. And besides, if I terminated you, it wouldn't exactly be the best look on your record."

The least I could do was let her go out legit. But she still brushed me off as if it was no big deal. "I already have a job lined up, but I appreciate you thinking about someone other than yourself for a change."

"What's your last name?"

She looked confused, pushing her salad around her plate as she asked, "Come again?"

I stared at her for a few seconds longer, knowing this little impromptu lunch that Leslie insisted on setting up was incredibly pointless before I asked again, "What's your last name? If you're supposedly carrying my child, the least I could do is know your last name."

She blushed, dropping her fork to her plate before she answered, "Oh. Right. It's Cooper."

"Hmm... Nicole Cooper. The gold-digger who's trying to ruin my reputation. Got it."

She smacked her teeth, snatching her napkin from her lap before tossing it on the table.

"Nobody forced you to have sex with me, Bryson. You chose, you wanted it, and you got it plus more." She even emphasized her point with a little belly rub that made *my* belly turn.

I was still pretty confident that she wasn't carrying my seed, but just the fact that she was encouraging the idea made me sick.

"No. *You* got it plus more from some unnamed mothafucka who's walkin' out here scot-free since you're so desperate to tie the baby to me and *my* legacy."

She picked her napkin back up, using it to dab the sides of her mouth as she tossed back, "Your words don't hurt me, Bryson. I know what happened and I know it's yours. That's all that matters when it comes to you and your precious little legacy."

I was desperate to know more, so I pried a little deeper. "Just out of curiosity, what's in it for you? I mean, other than the obvious... money, fifteen seconds of fame, maybe a reality show with a bunch of other thirsty bitches..."

"Excuse me?! I am *not* thirsty. If anything, you were thirsty when you tried to get me up to your hotel room."

My eyes rolled on their own. "There really wasn't much *trying* involved, but I'm not here to argue semantics. I wanna know your motive."

She took a sip of her water, shrugging as she answered, "I don't have a motive. I'm just here to get what I deserve. And you wouldn't have moved me out here if you didn't know that to be true."

"That didn't have anything to do with me. That was all my agent's doing simply because she didn't trust you to stay quiet, though I assured her you had nothing of substance from the jump." I still couldn't believe Leslie had gone through all the trouble of bringing the girl to town.

"Whatever. All I know is I'm here now and I already have shit that needs to get paid. So you gonna write the check or deposit the money into my account?"

I tried not to draw too much attention to us as I answered straight up, "I'm not giving you shit, Nicole."

She brushed me off again, looking at her nails as she replied, "That's not what Leslie said. *She* guaranteed $15,000 Pre-DNA test and another $20,000 contingent on it being confirmed as yours."

I choked on my water.

"She did *what*?!"

I just knew Leslie wouldn't sell me out without at least telling me first. But Nicole smiled confidently, leaning into the table to say, "That's right, baby. And mama has her eyes on a new pair of shoes and a bomb ass stylist. So I'll ask you again; are you gonna write me a check or deposit the money into my account?"

Kennedy

"Landon, we need to talk."

Walking around the house with the guilt from the night of my birthday gathering had officially become overwhelming. It probably would've been easier to have the conversation while the situation was still fresh, but there was no time like the present when it came to finally getting stuff off your chest.

He hardly looked concerned as he wiped his hands on a towel and turned the stove down to a simmer. "What's going on, babe?"

"I umm... I'm quitting my job." I figured that was the safest starting place.

His face scrunched with confusion as he asked, *"What?* Why? I thought you liked working with Bryson."

"I do. I... *did.* But we..." I choked on my words, pulling my bottom lip between my teeth as I tried to hold back the tears that were begging to be unleashed. It surprised me that I even had any left after crying every lonely night to sleep.

Now his concern fell in as he walked over to me, wrapping me in an embrace. "Babe, just tell me. What is it?"

I felt guilty for even letting him get this close, knowing my news would surely tear us apart. *"We... we...* we kinda developed umm... feelings for each other that were... far from professional."

He let me go, taking a step back as he said, "I don't understand."

A single tear sprang free without my permission and it hurt me even more when he reached in to wipe it.

"We... we *kissed*. And we... did some things that weren't appropriate. And I'm just so sorry, Landon." A few more tears joined the pity party, but this time I was forced to wipe them myself as Landon looked completely outdone.

His eyes were slanted and his arms were crossed as he asked, "What the fuck do you mean, *'things that weren't appropriate'*? *Did you...* did you fuck him, Kennedy?"

A fresh batch of tears dinged from the oven.

"No! I didn't have *that* kind of sex with him. I just... he just..."

He cut me off. "He just what? Fingered you?"

I shook my head no.

"Sucked a damn titty?"

No, again.

"Saw that pretty ass pussy of yours? *Tasted* that pretty ass pussy of yours?"

I froze.

His scowl became fierce as he digested the information. "How could you, Kennedy? *I*... I trusted you."

My emotions were everywhere as I admitted, "It was a mistake. A big, stupid mistake, and I'm just... I'm so sorry, Landon." I could hardly breathe, let alone speak as he watched me cry myself silly, completely unfazed.

"*A mistake?* You really expect me to believe that bullshit, Kennedy? I saw the way he looked at you the night of your birthday; the way you looked at him. And I told myself over and over again, 'Nah, man. We're talking about Kennedy. *My Kennedy.* She wouldn't even think to do something so.... *grimey.*'"

My breath caught in my chest once more as my eyes

120

became hazed by the overflow of tears.

"But you know what? I can't even blame you for that. It's my fault for being so damn naive when it came to you, believing that you were as perfect as you make everything seem."

My voice was hoarse as I told him, "I never meant to hurt you, Landon. I swear."

"Even if that wasn't your intention, that doesn't mean it didn't happen, Kennedy. I'm just so damn... *disappointed*."

My chest felt like it was caving in as I begged, "Landon, please..."

He put his hands up to stop me. "No, Kennedy! Don't *please* me. Don't *sorry* me. Don't do any of that shit! Just... let me figure this shit out for myself, alright?"

He made his way to the door, stuffing his feet into his tennis shoes as I asked with the little voice I had left, "What do you mean, figure it out?"

He yanked the door open as he answered, "This whole... relationship, the engagement, us in general. Just... give me some time."

I knew there was nothing I could say that would make him stay. So I let him go, closing and locking the door behind him before I fell to the ground and cried every drop of water I had left.

Bryson

I wasn't sure how I ended up back at the same strip club we went to on Kennedy's birthday, but it felt like a good idea to get rid of the stress of my day. After dealing with Nicole, and Leslie, *and* Kennedy, then playing yet another shitty game, blowing off some steam felt like the only thing that would keep me sane.

I strolled in through the back of the club so no one would see me, stopping by to dap up a few familiar faces before I found my designated section. I felt lonely as hell being in the strip club without company, but the solitude gave me a real chance to unwind and think some shit through; like what I was going to do if Nicole's baby was somehow miraculously mine. I knew the chance was slim to none, but all it took was a few percentage points for it to be true.

I was tempted to take a shot from the thought alone.

As I scanned the crowd, subconsciously thinking about who I wanted to give me a lap dance, my eyes landed on Landon who was all smiles as he smacked one of the strippers on the booty. Then he swept her money from the stage, putting it into a container before handing it to her. She smiled at him, exchanging some kind of energy that made him smack her on the ass again then follow her to the back.

My curiosity got the best of me, so I hopped up from my seat to follow them. Thankfully the security recognized me, letting me go past the prohibited area sign without a problem. I peeked into the first room which looked more like one of my high school locker rooms; except instead of basketball jerseys and shoes, there were platform heels and lingerie.

I continued my quest, peeking into the second room that turned out to be an office.

Maybe they didn't come back here.

"Shittt, Brandy."

My ears perked up on their own as I followed the noise to a third room. I looked inside and saw the same stripper from the stage on her knees sucking Landon's dick. My first instinct was to beat his ass for fuckin' Kennedy over, but that was just a bad headline waiting to happen. So instead, I cleared my throat as loud as I could to get their attention.

The stripper took notice before Landon did, and he had the nerve to look down at her wondering why she had stopped. She nodded her head my way and Landon's eyes flashed up to mine in shock. He pulled her from the ground while simultaneously pulling his pants up like I hadn't already figured out what was going on.

"What the fuck are you doing back here, man?!"

I shrugged. "Self-guided tour, I guess. Was actually thinking about investing in something like this. It seems to be pretty... *profitable*." I looked over to the stripper who was beyond embarrassed as she fixed the little bit of clothes she had on and darted out of the room.

While Landon kept working on his belt, I kept running my mouth. "You know, it's kinda funny that I caught you like this, bro. I mean, while Kennedy thinks you're here working to save up for the wedding and shit, you're really in here gettin' your dick sucked every night. And to think she actually felt guilty about the little shit she did with me."

He had the nerve to get all riled up like I'd be even remotely intimidated. "Mothafucka, I should beat your ass for touching my woman!"

"Should you? *Eh*... maybe. But after this, it probably wouldn't be in your best interest. For one, the only ass gettin' beat would be yours. And for two, even if you *did* win, I could still tell Kennedy what I saw. So do you really wanna get your ass beat and get your girl snatched? I have a hard time believing that."

He wore the smuggest little smirk as he tossed out, "Kennedy's at home crying over me right now. She's never gonna leave me."

I couldn't help but bruise his little ego. "You wanna know why she's with you? Because she's loyal. But you just broke that, man. So now there's nothing holding her back from going after what she really wants, which I can already assure you is me." I thought about dropping her direct quote just to fuck with him even more.

"You really think she's gonna believe you over me? Even if you did have something with her, she's getting away from you solely because she *loves* me. I can go home right now and tell her I forgive her for that shit with you and she'll be sucking my dick just like Brandy was."

Now this cocky little mothafucka is gettin' on my nerves....

"Bro, I swear to God. If you even *think* about pullin' some shit like that on Kennedy, I will kill you with my bare hands." Even if we weren't on the best terms, I would forever consider her a friend. And friends protect friends at all costs.

I almost snapped when he brushed me off, but instead I just bit the inside of my cheek to hear him out. "Whatever, Bryson. You're all talk. That's how all y'all ball players are. Think you can just do whatever you want to whoever you want. Stay away from me and mine, bruh. We good."

I couldn't believe he really thought I was just going

to let his sorry ass go back to Kennedy with no repercussions. Even if she didn't end up with me, Landon was no longer an option.

But I knew talking to him anymore than I already had was useless. So I acted like I no longer cared, tossing my hands up and leaving the room.

I watched Kennedy mosey around the boutique, sifting through the racks of clothes as she tried to find a few things for me to add to my closet before a new stylist would take her place. This time around, I refused to be a part of the hiring process, so I could pretty much assume that Leslie had hired the ugliest person she could find.

Hell, she probably hired a man.

But that was the least of my concerns. I was busy trying to figure out how to ask Kennedy about Landon without sounding like I was hatin'.

If Landon hadn't said anything - which I could pretty much assume he hadn't -, then it would probably seem like I was just trying to start trouble and that was hardly the case. I wanted the best for Kennedy, I cared about her, and she deserved much better than a fool like Landon.

So when she took the clothes to the register to checkout, tossing them on the counter, I casually asked, "So... how are you and Landon doing?"

To no surprise, she kept it short. "We're fine."

"So he... came home last night?"

She turned to me with an attitude speckled with confusion. "Of course he did. Why wouldn't he have come home, Bryson?"

I shrugged, trying not to spill all the beans at once. "I don't know. I just... you don't mind him working nights at the strip club? Being around all those ass-shakin', half-naked women?" Maybe laying the facts on the table first would make the news less alarming.

She still wasn't catching my drift, using my card to pay for the clothes as she tossed back, "It's a means to an end."

I signed the receipt, grabbing the bags as I worked to get my point across. "*End*. That's exactly what I was thinking too. Like how you need to *end* your engagement with Landon."

Oops.

Her eyes went wide as she shot me a scowl from the store all the way to the car. She waited until we were in route back to my house to respond, "You have got to be kidding me, Bryson. I mean, where do you even come up with this stuff?"

I tried to keep my eyes on the road as I explained, "Kennedy, *I*... look, I know you probably won't believe any of what I tell you but just hear me out, alright?" I watched from my peripheral as she rolled her eyes but nodded her head, allowing me to go on. "I was at the club last night, and *I*... I saw Landon with a girl; with one of the girls."

She brushed me off. "Well he works there, Bryson. I'm sure he has to interact from time-to-time."

"Nah, Kenn. Not like that. She was giving him some umm... some sloppy toppy."

She turned in her seat to look at me. "Sloppy.... *toppy*? Is this some kind of joke, Bryson? Cause I'm really not in the mood today."

"I'm not joking, Kennedy. I saw it with my own two eyes; her on her knees in front of Landon and I can guarantee she wasn't checkin' his prostate."

She was more annoyed than convinced as she sarcastically asked, "So you want me to believe that some stripper was giving Landon head in the middle of the club for you to see? Oh. *Okay.* Got it."

"No. I found them. In the back."

She tossed her hands up as she turned to the window, completely outdone by the conversation.

"*Oh,* so you were looking for something to be wrong with him? Even better."

I tried to make her understand my motives as I explained, "Kennedy, I went back there for you. To look out... *for you.*"

"And instead, you just threw a new wrench at me to make my life a little worse than you've already made it. Thanks a lot, Bryson. You're a class act."

"I'm serious, Kenn. I could tell he was on some slick shit, so I went back there to see what was going on, and... that was what I found. So you can be mad at me if you want to, but I needed you to know the truth."

Her demeanor completely changed as she turned back my way, leaning over the middle console to get in my face. "*The truth?* You wanna talk about the truth? Fine. Let's talk about how you *truthfully* have a child on the way." *Wait what?* "Yeah, I met your little baby mama. She actually hired me to be her stylist."

That's the position she was talking about?

"Kennedy, you didn't..."

She fell back in her seat with a smirk like she was actually proud of that shit.

"Yes, I did. Because regardless of our past dealings, I still have bills to pay. So while you can go around playing with people's minds and hearts, the rest of us have priorities to align."

For some reason, the first thing that came to mind to respond was, "It's not mine."

"Well then why is she here?"

There was really no reason to lie about it, so I told

her straight up, "Leslie did that. Leslie guaranteed her some money which I'm assuming she gave you part of. But that's the last of it, so I would advise you not to accept the position."

She shrugged. "Already signed a contract."

"Kenn..."

"Don't *Kenn* me now, Bryson. The decision was mine to make so I made it. Now I appreciate the opportunity you gave me to work for you, but I'm done with this. *I'm...* I'm done with you."

Kennedy

I watched with skepticism as Landon got dressed for his shift at the club. The bad bitch in me wanted to pull every last stitch of his clothes from the closet and burn them like Angela Bassett in *Waiting to Exhale*, but I wasn't quite ready to get arrested for arson until I had definite proof that Bryson had actually been telling the truth.

It shouldn't have surprised me when Bryson decided to drop the bomb of Landon's apparent infidelity on my last day working for him. It was like he just couldn't come to terms with what was really happening; that we were *really* done with each other. It wasn't like we frequented the same places or ran in any of the same circles, so I probably wouldn't ever see him again.

At least, I hoped I would never see him again.

Because every time I saw him, there was a rush of emotions that wondered what if, a feeling of guilt from getting so deeply involved, a curiosity that honestly led me to believe there was some truth to his actions beyond the constant seduction and manipulation, *and*...

"Alright, babe. I'll be back tonight. No need to wait up, though. I'm sure it'll be a later one than usual since we have a couple Philly players hosting."

I never purposely waited up; it was usually because I had too much on my mind to go to sleep.

But tonight...

Tonight would be different.

I was on a mission.

I tried to sound as normal as I could when I replied, "Oh. Okay. Well I'll just see you in the morning then."

Before he headed to the door, he leaned in to give me a kiss on the cheek. He probably thought he was doing me a favor by being nice to me after my guilty admission, but we'd be finding out who was really the bad guy tonight.

"Kennedy, you look ridiculous," Chloe whispered as I pulled my hat low over my eyes.

I thought the outfit was kind of cute; my black NY fitted cap giving an edgy look to the black leather skin-tight pants and black tank covered by a black blazer, then complemented with a pair of black high-heeled sandals. But of course, Chloe was just being a hater as usual.

I probably could've pulled the mission off alone, but something about having an accomplice made it real even though I hadn't given her all the details of the situation. She ran her mouth way too much for me to tell it all.

I kept my head down as I paid the cover charge and Chloe did the same. Then we entered the club, trying not to look the least bit suspicious, though it immediately felt like all eyes were on us. The crowd was relatively thick, but I assumed that had something to do with the slew of basketball players Landon mentioned being in attendance.

Speaking of Landon...

I looked towards the stage and saw him at his normal post, observing the crowd before turning back to the dancer and using a push broom to collect her earnings as she finished her set. He tossed her a towel to wipe the pole down before helping her from the stage and handing her the money-filled container.

Well this looks nor...

"Oh, hell no! Did you see Landon touch that girl?!"

My eyes were already beaming in their direction when Chloe spoke. The girl was smiling her little ass off as Landon followed her to the back.

What the fuck?

"Kennedy, did you hear me?!"

I tried to stay calm as I responded, "I heard you, Chloe. I'm gonna go see what's going on. Stay here, alright?"

I didn't have time to wait on an actual response as I was already headed their way. I was almost past the prohibited area when a big, burly man stepped in front of me.

"Whoa, little lady. This area is for employees only."

Shit.

Think, Kennedy!

I put on the sexiest voice I could muster and told him, "I... umm. I'm new here. It's my first night."

He seemed intrigued, crossing his arms over his massive chest to ask, "Oh word? What's your name, sweetie?"

"That's for me to know and you to find out... *big daddy.*"

I cringed on the inside knowing my real father would kill me if he ever heard me calling some random man that name. But the gigantic man only smiled, a genuine one I hardly expected from a guy in his position.

"I hear you, mama. Well good luck tonight. It's a lotta money out there to be made if you know what you're doing."

"*Th...* thank you," I stumbled as I squeezed past him.

The back was loud with all of the ladies going on and on about how they better get picked for the baller's section. I figured if Landon was doing dirt, he probably wouldn't be doing it with all this company. So I continued my way to the back, passing a few offices before I found exactly what I was looking for.

"Brandy told me it was big, so I had to see for myself."

He let out an unrecognizable laugh as he replied, *"I can assure you that Brandy wasn't lying, baby girl."*

I had already heard enough.

I stepped in the room, announcing my presence with a question. "Oh, you can?"

He muffed the girl to the side, approaching me with short, urgent steps. "Kennedy! *What the…* what are you doing here, babe?"

I remained calm, refusing to cause a scene. "Just passing through, checking on my *fiancé*. But I see I should've done this little visit earlier so I could've figured out how much of a fraud you are."

"*Fraud*? Kennedy, it's not what it looks like. I swear. We were just..."

I held my hand up to stop him. "Landon, just save it, alright? Let me remember you as the good person you were, not the bullshitter you'll turn yourself into if you say another word."

He looked on the verge of tears as he put his arms around my waist to say, "We all make mistakes, Kennedy. *I…* I fucked up just like you."

"Correction. You were *actively* fucking up for who knows how long and only feel remorseful because you got caught. I was brutally honest with you about my indiscretions. So like I said, save the bullshit. I'm done with this."

I tried to walk off, but he caught me by my wrist. "Kennedy, please. We can work this out. We can fix this."

134

His eyes held so much promise, his words sounded so sincere. But as I looked behind him at the girl who, for whatever reason, felt the need to stay and listen in on our whole conversation, I realized that I would be doing a lot more than settling if I took him back.

So I took a deep breath before I confidently pushed out, "Landon... it's been real."

His eyes zeroed in on me as I turned to walk away, out of the room and past the big burly man from before. I went back to where I had left Chloe, and of course she wasn't there.

Damnit!

"Kennedy! Kennedy, over here!"

I looked towards the VIP sections and there she was, yelling over the shoulder of a guy I recognized as Wes. I was more than ready to go, but I certainly didn't want to knock her game. So I kept my head low as I headed her way.

Once I made it up the short set of stairs, Chloe bombarded me with a shot glass.

"It's Wes's birthday, so take the shot!"

Wes stood nearby smiling as he lifted a shot glass of his own. I knew it probably wasn't a good idea to start drinking in my current semi-frazzled state, but one shot wouldn't hurt. So I clinked glasses with Wes, tossing it back and embracing the burn of the situation.

Bryson

I woke up to the sound of my doorbell ringing non-stop. I grabbed my phone to take a peek at the time and only found a slew of missed calls from Wes, probably trying to get in touch since I hadn't shown up to his birthday party. After what had gone down with Landon, I didn't think it was a good idea for me to show my face at the club again so soon. But I wasn't ready to let Wes in on that situation quite yet, so I chose to just avoid it altogether.

The doorbell rang a few times more, reminding me why I had woken up in the first place and forcing me to climb out of bed to tend to it. Since it was late at night, I was cautious as I peeked through the side window. But once I figured out who it was, I opened it immediately.

Kennedy laughed her way from Wes's arms to mine as she slurred, "Hiii, Bryson."

I caught her, stumbling back a little from the unexpected looseness of her frame.

"What the hell is going on?"

Wes had the nerve to laugh as he answered, "She got wayyy too lit, bruh. And I offered to give her a ride home, but she said she wanted to come here."

Kennedy let out another laugh as I sat her down on the entryway bench.

"*She did?*" Now that surprised me.

He patted me on the shoulder with another laugh. "Yeah, man. So I listened to the lady and brought her here. Now if you don't need anything else, I'd love to tend to her friend who's waiting for me in the whip."

Ohh, that's what this is about.

"Nah, we're good, bro. Thanks for getting her here safely."

"No problem, B-Money. Y'all be good now."

I watched as he jogged from my doorstep back to his car before I closed the door. Then I turned around and saw that Kennedy was nowhere to be found.

Where the hell did she go?

I heard a door shut upstairs, and though I didn't know how she could've made it up there so fast, I climbed the stairs two-by-two to catch up with her. I passed a bunch of open guest room doors until I landed on the only door that was shut; my bedroom.

Not now, Kenn...

I braced myself before I opened the door, not sure what I'd be walking in on. I didn't see her right away. But as I went further into the room, I noticed a bump moving under the comforter.

"Kennedy, what are you doing?" I asked as I approached the bed, stepping on a pile of her discarded clothes.

Her voice was muffled as she rolled around on the mattress. "I've always wondered what these sheets felt like. I mean, I got to see them all the time. But to feel them on my bare skin... all one thousand threads of Egyptian cotton. *Mmm...*"

I sat on the edge of the bed, pulling the comforter back to see her face.

Damn, she's faded as hell.

Her eyes sat low and slanted as she smiled when they finally landed on me. "Come onnnn, Bryson. Come lay with me."

I scooted a little closer, pushing her hair from her forehead as I told her, "Kennedy, that's not a good idea and you know it. You're drunk. *Way* drunk. You can stay here, but I'm going to the guest room."

She looked defeated as I tossed the comforter back over her face. It took everything in me to leave her alone, especially knowing there wasn't much covering her body under the comforter. But there was no way I was going to take advantage of her current state. People go down over shit like that way too often and I already had enough going wrong in my corner to risk another case.

My hand was on the doorknob when I felt something smack me in the back of the head. I turned around, picking it up from the ground as I said, "Really, Kenn? Your panties as a parting gift?"

She giggled, pulling the comforter up to her chin as she replied, "Just a little reminder of what you're missing out on by sleeping in the guest room. Guess I'll just have to... do it myself. All over these perfect ass sheets."

I took a deep breath as I tried to digest the idea of Kennedy's innocent ass playing with herself.

And that pretty ass pus...

"Kenn. Scale from one to ten. How drunk are you?"

She giggled once more as she answered, "Twelve." *Shit.* "Mmm... I feel so damn good. And wet. *And...*"

I fell against the door as I watched her kick the comforter off, covering my eyes like I was a kid watching the nasty part of the movie with my parents. "Quit it, Kenn. *Shit,* at least let me leave first."

Peeking through my fingers was a bad idea as she tossed her head back and demanded, "Watch me, Brysonnnn. Watch me... *mmm...*"

Damn, she is wet.

Her fingers glossed over as she strummed them against her swollen pearl. I was hypnotized as I watched her pleasure herself. My dick was painfully hard, and I...

"*Shit, Kennedy.* What are you doing to me?"

139

Her eyes shut even tighter as she belted, "Fuckkkk, I'm about to…"

Oh my God.

It felt like the gates of Heaven were opening right in front of me as I watched Kennedy have an orgasm. Of course, it wasn't the first time. But the fact that I had nothing to do with it definitely heightened the moment.

When she finally came down from her high, she wore the cutest little satisfied smirk, and all I could do was stand there in awe.

Her eyes cracked open just slightly as she tossed out, "Goodnight, Bryson." Then she dozed off to sleep.

My dreams were embarrassingly vivid as I unconsciously made use of Kennedy's little pre-bedtime show. I still couldn't believe she had gone so far. But I was honestly impressed by how much freedom she let herself have for a change, though I wasn't sure how it related to everything else. Like how she ended up with Wes in the first place, and what was going on with her and Landon, and why she had insisted on coming here instead of going home. But those were all questions that could be answered when I went back to the master bedroom.

I made up the bed in the guest room, straightening up the little I had rearranged before I made my way a few doors down. I opened the door and the room looked completely untouched, everything in place like she had never been there at all. The only reason I knew I wasn't dreaming was because of the note left in the middle of the bed, right next to the pair of panties she had slingshotted at me.

I smiled to myself, rubbing the thin, lacy fabric

between my fingers as I read the note.

Some women simply don't unveil every personality trait the first couple of times they meet someone. Some of us like to keep things a mystery until the friendship develops. You know, allow things to unfold. ;)
Thanks for the hospitality and enjoy the gift,
XOXO Kenn

Kennedy

The call came in before I could even make it back to my apartment.

I smiled when I saw his name pop up, though I had absolutely no idea what I was doing when it came to him. I knew my moves had been somewhat reckless, at least from what I remembered. But at this point, it was too late to take them back.

"Hello?"

"Kennedy Wilson. Thank you."

I blushed unashamedly, knowing he couldn't possibly see it through the phone.

"What'd I do?" I asked teasingly as I turned into the parking lot of my apartment complex.

He groaned into the phone as if he was remembering every detail that was honestly a blur to me. "Your performance last night was... impeccable. *Five stars.* Now what do I need to do to earn an encore?"

A laugh boiled over before I could contain it.

"There won't be an encore, Bryson. It was just a... what'd you call it? Heat of the moment thing."

He let out a little laugh of his own as he said, "Well can I at least take you to lunch so we can... talk about it? Maybe not the fine details of you begging me to watch, but at least the motive."

Damn, I said all that?

I quickly thought it over. And no matter how warm the concept made me feel, the little ounce of control I had left told me otherwise.

"Bryson, I don't think that would be a good idea. Things aren't exactly the clearest for me right now and I... probably shouldn't have shown up to your place last night with all my baggage."

I was beyond grateful that he hadn't taken advantage of me, though I highly doubted I would've regretted that part of it.

He sighed into the phone, not quite disappointedly but still holding a different kind of weight as he explained, "Kenn, I'm your friend. Friends take care of friends, no matter how much of my willpower you drained by playing with your pussy in the middle of my bed."

Hearing him say it out loud caused a rush of embarrassment to run over me.

"I'm sorry, Bryson."

"Don't be. It's all good. Just let me know when you're ready to talk, alright? I'll be here."

Though I had told Bryson more than once to his face that he wasn't shit to me, I knew better now. He may have been a little manipulative in general, but he had certainly been an ally when it came to this particular situation. He didn't have to open the door, he didn't have to respect me, *he didn't have to...*

"Thank you. I gotta go. I'll... talk to you later?"

I could feel his smile through the phone as he said, "Looking forward to it."

"So... did you fuck him or what?"

I thought about tossing my freshly broken off piece of bread at Chloe's forehead for asking, but instead I flipped it back on her. "Did you fuck Wes?"

She rolled her eyes like the answer was obvious.

"Come on now, Kennedy. Is that even a real question? Of course I did. And he was... he was *alright*."

"*Alright*?"

She took a sip of her martini - *her third if we were keeping count* - as she broke it down. "I'd give him a... B overall. *A+* effort, *B+* length, *C-* Stamina."

I took a sip of my water, still trying to fight the hangover from the night before as I asked, "Ahh, so Mr. Wes was a quick pumper?"

She swatted a hand at me. "Quick is an understatement. But we're not here for that. We're here to find out what happened with you and Bryson. So spill it."

I sighed deeply as I gave her the most honest version I could without saying too much. "Nothing happened, Chloe. He was a complete gentleman; slept in a different room and everything."

It still surprised me that between us two, he was actually the one who had made the responsible decision.

"What?! You must really be in love with Landon if you didn't let Bryson hit that."

Just the mention of both names in the same sentence made me cringe.

"*I*... I do love Landon. A piece of me will always love Landon. But he... he's not who I thought he was."

The irony of the situation still blew my mind. How he tried to belittle me for my honesty like he wasn't out here pulling shit on the side.

Ugh.

As I was busy in my own thoughts, Chloe kept her eyes fixated on my face as if she was trying to get a read on me. "Hmm... are you sure about that? Or did it just take someone else coming along for you to realize it?"

"Maybe both? I don't know, Chloe. This is still new for me."

"I understand. I still can't believe he was fucking around with those girls at the club, though. She wasn't even cute. *And* her butt was fake."

I couldn't help but laugh at that. "I know, right? It like... wasn't even shakin'."

We laughed together as my phone began to ring. I picked it up from the table, getting a closer look at who the call was coming from.

Nicole.

I had honestly kind of forgotten about her. But now that Bryson had been a friend to me, it was only fair that I did the same.

"Hello?"

She sang into the phone, "Heyyyy Kennedy. So I'm at the mall looking at some pieces and I was thinking you should probably join me. I mean, since you're my stylist and all."

Chloe gave me the, *'who is that'* look, and I tried to answer with my emphasis, "Actually, *Nicole*. I don't think I'll be able to work for you after all. It's just... conflict of interest."

I still didn't know if she was really carrying Bryson's baby. But either way, it was too close for comfort.

She smacked her teeth as she asked, "Conflict of interest? What does that even mean?"

I broke it down as simply as I could. "It means... I can't work for you."

I pulled the phone away from my ear as she yelled, "But you signed a contract!"

There was really no reason for me to get out of character, so I remained calm as I told her, "And now I'm breaking it."

"Bitch, I'll sue your ass into the ground."

Her use of expletives tickled me. She was surely a

fan of old tricks if she thought dropping the B-word was going to get me emotionally-invested in the conversation.

"Let's be real, Nicole. How much sense would that make? I mean, for one... you can't really afford it. For two, would you rather me show up and make you look like crap? I think not."

She grunted before she spewed, "Whatever, Kennedy. If you don't wanna work for me, fine! You weren't that good anyway."

But you hired me so...

"O... kay, Nicole. Be well. Good luck with the pregnancy."

She growled into the phone before hanging up and Chloe immediately jumped into action. "Do we need to ride out on that bitch? She was rude as hell."

Though I always brushed off the idea of having friends, Chloe was definitely as ride-or-die as they came. "Nah, it's all good. Let's just focus on the positive. Like your next step with Mr. Wes."

Bryson

"So I think I deserve a token of appreciation for delivering Kennedy to your front door like a Hot 'N Ready pizza."

I laughed Wes off as I wiped my face with my towel before tossing it over my shoulder after practice. I still hadn't gotten a chance to get the full story out of Kennedy, so I was counting on Wes to give me the details.

I waited until we settled in at our respective lockers to ask, "How'd that shit happen anyway?"

He took a swig from his water bottle before he answered, "According to Chloe, she and her dude got into it over some shit at the club."

Of course this dude was pillow talkin'...

"Oh word?"

I changed out of my practice jersey into a regular t-shirt while I listened to him answer, "Yeah. And Chloe was already chillin' with me when all that shit settled, so Kennedy came and joined us. Took a few shots too many, and next thing you know she was begging me to take her to your crib."

"Begging you?" I hardly saw Kennedy as the begging type.

Though she did beg you to watch her...

"Begging, bruh. I'm assuming her ol' man was probably gonna be at the crib tryna get her back. And since Chloe was without a doubt coming home with me, you were her first option."

The explanation made total sense no matter how surprising it was that she had thought of me as a safe place to go.

"Hmmm… that's interesting."

"Nah, what's interesting is how many positions you had her fine ass in before the sun came up."

I brushed him off. "Chill, bro. We didn't even do anything."

He didn't even pretend to be convinced as he said, "Bryson, I've known you a few years now and I have a hard time believing that shit. Unless, you... *awww shit*."

"What?"

He eyed me for a minute before he asked, "You really care about her, don't you?"

"Most definitely."

He looked borderline disappointed. "Damn, so y'all really didn't do anything?"

I shook my head no, though clips of her in the middle of my bed had been on repeat ever since.

"You better be careful, man. One second you care about her, the next second you'll be in love."

My heart damn near skipped a beat. I had never been a fan of the L word; at least not in a serious manner.

"*In love*? Nah, man. It's not even like that." Though I cared for Kennedy quite a bit, I hardly saw love being the case.

"Sounds all fine and dandy now, but don't be surprised when cupid comes and bites you in the ass when you least expect it."

"Big bro, you gotta let me have these kicks. I mean, ever since you've been on your grown and sexy thanks to that stylist of yours, you probably don't even have the time to give these babies the attention they deserve."

I gave my little brother Miles a smack to the side of his head to knock some sense into him as I dragged him out of my closet. He was visiting for the first week of his summer break before he planned on flying down to Atlanta to see his girlfriend.

"Off limits, bro. You know that. And besides, my stylist doesn't control all my moves. Not anymore at least."

I still became annoyed with the idea that Kennedy had quit her job with me to take one with Nicole. But the fact that she was at least talking to me now somewhat made up for it.

"Yeah right. After I saw you in those tight ass pants in that interview you did, I knew whoever she was must have you wrapped around her finger."

Damn, was it that obvious?

I brushed him off. "Nah, she just had a vision. And you know how Leslie is about my image, so I had to follow the rules."

He eyed me suspiciously before he followed me out of the room and down the stairs. "Mmhmm. How bad is she? Be real."

I dug in my pocket and pulled out my phone, scrolling through my *Instagram* app to find her profile. When I found one of my favorites, a picture I had actually screenshotted to save in my phone, I handed it to him.

"Damnnnnnn. She *is* bad."

I could tell he was scrolling to other pictures, so I snatched the phone back from him as I told him, "I'm tellin' Ava on you."

"Aye, man. Even my girl can appreciate a beautiful woman when she sees one."

I knew that was a stretch, but I let it slide.

151

I was just getting ready to ask him about his final grades for the semester when the doorbell rang. I wasn't expecting anyone, so I gave the nod to Miles to answer it for me and run clearance. Then I stood by the stairs to listen in.

His voice took a different tone as he said, "Can I help you with something, ma?"

Should've known it was a girl...

"Hi. I was... looking for Bryson. Is he here?"

Kennedy?

Miles leaned away from the door to make sure it was cool, and I waved for him to let her in.

"Yeah, he's here. Come on in, ma."

He opened the door further to let her past, shamelessly checking her out as she went around him. Behind her back, he gave me two thumbs up then jokingly wiped his mouth.

"Kenn. What's up, girl?" I strolled over to her, pulling her into a hug just so I could get a whiff of her always pleasant scent.

"Well I called myself doing one of those *in-the-area* visits friends do, but I didn't account for company. My apologies."

I quickly assured her, "This knucklehead is hardly company. Kennedy, this is my little brother Miles. Miles, Kennedy."

I couldn't believe the little smirk he put on to pull her into a hug of his own. He peeked over her shoulder to taunt me and I mouthed, *"I'm telling Ava."*

"It's good to meet you, Miles. I hope you're nothing like your brother," she teased.

"Not in the slightest, ma. He's more of a Beyoncé. I'm just Solange."

Kennedy busted out laughing as she stood on her tippy-toes to wrap her arm around his shoulder and say,

"Well I just so happen to like Solange, particularly for her fashion sense. So you're good in my book."

Miles flashed me the biggest smile as he teased, "You hear that, Bryson? I'm good in her book."

Instead of giving Miles's antics any attention, I directed it all to Kennedy. "You want something to drink? Miles has already eaten the fridge bare. So if you're hungry, we'll have to go out somewhere."

"I'm actually good. But do you think we could talk... *alone?*"

Miles looked at me for an answer until he realized what she had said. "Oh. Oh! My bad. I'm going. But if y'all go get something to eat, I'm coming with. A brotha is mad hungry."

Kennedy laughed again as I shoved him towards the stairs. Then I led her to the living room as she gushed, "He's adorable."

"Don't let him hear that shit. He likes 'em older." Even though I knew he had Ava, I still wasn't going to let him get too comfortable with Kennedy.

She fell onto the couch, pulling her shoes off as she replied, "Well with that natural charm, I'm sure he pulls 'em by the boatload."

I made myself comfortable next to her, not hesitating to pull her feet into my lap and give 'em a rub down. "He's actually going to see his little girlfriend when he leaves here in a few days. She's a pro basketball player down in Atlanta."

Her eyes closed as she adjusted to the pressure. "Awwwww. Like *Love & Basketball?*"

Why does everyone always reference that shit?

I laughed as I replied, "Yeah, something like that. But enough about them. What's up with you?"

"Nothin' much. What's up with you?" she joked.

"Kenn, you are so cheesy. But really though, what's

153

going on?"

Her whole demeanor seemed to change as she pulled her feet from my hands. "I umm... I canceled my contract with Nicole."

Now that caught me off-guard. Kennedy had made such a big deal before about how she had bills to pay. And even though I knew Nicole wouldn't have been able to pay her for long, she certainly had enough money for at least a couple paychecks.

"Word? Why'd you do that?"

She shrugged, her eyes on her hands as she twiddled her thumbs and answered, "I don't know. I guess after seeing your true colors the other night, it just felt like the right thing to do."

"*My true colors*? Kennedy, I've been real with you from the jump." Though things had gotten a little cloudy from time-to-time, there had never been an instance of me deliberately selling her lies.

"Tell me then. Straight up. Is she really pregnant with your baby?"

I released a heavy sigh before I honestly answered, "As bluntly as possible, unless she masterminded some crazy shit like poking a hole in my condom collection or somethin' like that, then the chances are slim to none. But we still have to wait for the DNA test to be a thousand percent sure."

The whole process was exhausting, but I was grateful that Leslie handled the in-person dealings with Nicole so I wouldn't have to anymore.

"And when are you gonna do that?"

I was literally counting down the days of the last, "Two weeks."

"So I have to wait a whole two weeks until I can find out how *outstanding* you are?"

Wait a minute... what?

———

154

She blushed as she casted her eyes back down to her hands. "I mean, I'm not getting any on the regular these days, and a girl can only do so much with her hands before she gets early onset arthritis."

I snatched her feet back into a hold, applying pressure in just the right spot to make her head fly back.

"Kennedy, I'm a strong, youthful man with a strong sex game. Why are you wasting orgasms on your hands?"

"Because your strong ass has a possible. So until then... Little Miss Kenn has to keep herself occupied."

Her teasing was way too cute.

I watched her eyes roll to the back of her head as I did some teasing of my own on her feet.

"You gonna wait for me?"

Her answer came out as more of a moan than anything. "*Yeah*... I'll wait for you."

I felt giddy as hell as I sat there thinking of the possibilities. And just when I was getting ready to go into the details of how good I was going to make it for her, I heard Miles yell from the stairs, "Y'all so nasty!"

Kennedy

I should've stayed away a little longer.

That's all I kept thinking as I quietly shut the front door, the resounding sound of clothes being pulled from the rack in the closet serving as background noise.

Landon and I - *more me than Landon* – had come to the conclusion that it was best that he'd move out of the apartment we shared. For whatever reason he was convinced that our actions were equal meaning they practically neutralized one another.

Hardly the case.

After talking to Brandy - though a confrontation was more than tempting -, I found out the *whole* truth. And let's just say, Landon was lucky to still have clothes to pack. But I was no longer bitter, or angry, or… any of that. In fact, I felt refreshed because I was actually starting a new chapter of my life.

I leaned against the doorframe of the closet as he stuffed his clothes in a box, similar to the way Bryson had insisted on stuffing his clothes in his suitcase long ago.

Men.

"Hey. Can I… help you?"

He peeked up from his box with tired eyes to nod his head yes. I looked in the box and decided it was best to dump it and start over.

"Damn, babe. I've been working hard to fill that box."

I was already busy sorting the clothes by style. "Well

you can get triple the stuff in it if you take your time to fold everything. But don't worry, that's what I'm here for," I replied with a smile. He returned a smile of his own, the creases of his face almost looking new as if he hadn't smiled in days.

I continued sorting but could feel Landon's eyes on me as he watched me work.

"Aren't you gonna help?"

He snapped out of his daze to respond, "Oh! Yeah... *yeah.* I was just... *damn*, what happened to us, Kennedy? I mean, we were good together, weren't we? *You...* you really loved me, didn't you?"

Not now...

I began to fold a few shirts, explaining things to him as honestly as I could. "Of course I did, Landon. And I still do. It just... *we just...* didn't work. Obviously, considering we both stepped out on our relationship."

Saying it out loud gave me chills. I mean, I had already acknowledged my wrong-doings, but there was no removing the guilt I still felt for letting things go so far.

Landon's voice took a softer, pleading tone as he stated, "I felt like I was losing you, babe. You were so busy with your new job, spending all that time with Bryson, and I just... my insecurities about it led me to test out my skills on other women. But it was a mistake, Kennedy. I swear it was a... *mistake.*" His voice cracked as he finished his spiel.

I know this fool isn't about to cry...

I peeked up to confirm my suspicions and immediately had to cast my eyes back down to the clothes.

"Landon, I believe you. And to be quite honest, I forgive you. It's no longer something for me to dwell on. Everything happens for a reason."

I could feel him staring at me as he finally confessed, "I'm not ready to let you go, Kennedy."

And there it was.

The single tear that crushed my core.

"I'm…" *Shit, don't look at him.* "I'm sorry, Landon. But you made that decision when you decided to mess around with those damn strippers."

He silently wiped his tears and I tried to calm my own emotions so that I could finish helping him with his clothes. I folded a few things, gently laying them in the box just as my phone began to ring. I picked it up and saw it was a *FaceTime* call from Bryson. I looked over to Landon who had all eyes on me, waiting to see both who it was and if I was actually going to take it. Without an explanation, I left him in the closet and headed first to the living room, but then outside of the front door knowing how unpredictable Bryson could be.

Once the call connected, Bryson's smile grew, and I couldn't ignore the warmth my skin felt from that single motion.

"Kennedy Wilson, what's good?"

"Are you gonna keep rubbing my singleness in my face?"

"Yeah, until I can make you Kennedy Harris."

The guilty little smile he wore made me laugh.

"You play too much."

He let out a few laughs of his own. "But nah, I was calling to see if you wanted to go bowling with Miles and I tonight. He insisted on inviting you. I think Chloe and Wes are coming too."

Going out with Bryson and company didn't sound like the worst idea in the book, especially after the still-pending drama with Landon.

I couldn't help but tease, "Miles insisted on inviting me or you did?"

His guilty little smile returned as he answered, "Miles... and I. We both did. So you comin' or what?"

"Yeah, I'll come."

His excitement radiated through the phone.

"Cool. I'll pick you up around ten."

"Umm... actually, can I just meet you at your house? Landon's still here." The last thing I needed was a showdown between the two.

He appeared a little withdrawn as he responded, "*Oh*... yeah. That's cool."

"What's the matter?"

He was quiet for a moment, looking past the screen before he finally asked, "*He*... he didn't try anything, did he? I know he still wants you, Kenn.*"

Though I could also pretty much tell that was the case, the last thing I needed was Bryson getting involved. So I answered, "Nah, he's been cool. I'm helping him pack."

Now he looked flat-out annoyed.

"Kenn, you're helping your ex-fiancé who cheated on you pack his shit?"

It sounded a little far-fetched when spoken out loud, but I quickly reminded him, "Technically, I cheated on him first... remember?"

His smile was back as he licked his lips, "Mmmhmmmm. I sure do. And I can't wait to refresh my memory."

I bit my bottom lip, trying to stifle a grin of my own. "Whatever, Bryson. I'm gonna go finish helping him. I'll be over later."

"Looking forward to it, baby."

Shit, I'm in trouble.

I walked back into the house on cloud nine just as Landon was carrying the box of clothes into the living room.

―――

160

"Oh, you finished it by yourself?"

His smile was halfhearted as he answered, "Yeah. Figured I should start getting used to it. You know, the whole *alone* thing."

"Landon..."

He instantly looked furious as he spewed, "What, Kennedy? I mean damn, you couldn't even wait for me to move out before you started hookin' up with ol' boy? What is it about him anyway? His money can only go so far."

I tried not to get pissed as I assured him, "We're not hookin' up, Landon."

Partially true...

He took the few steps over to me, getting right in my face to say, "Not... *yet*. That's what you meant, right? *Not yet?*"

I stepped past him, grabbing my purse from the couch before heading to the door. "Whatever, Landon. I don't have to explain myself to you. I'm leaving. And while you're at it, feel free to speed up this whole *moving-out* process."

Bryson

"You're early."

I smiled down on Kennedy as she rolled her eyes and strolled past me into the house. I closed the door and took the few strides to catch up with her, pulling her back by the wrist.

"Hey. What's wrong with you?"

She looked me dead in my eyes to ask, "Do you have any alcohol here?"

I frowned, wanting to pull her into an embrace but not wanting to overstep since I could pretty much assume her attitude had something to do with Landon.

"Damn. That bad, huh?"

She looked exhausted as she replied, "No. I'm just... I don't know what I'm doing, Bryson. I'm used to being so in control, and right now everything feels so... *not.*"

I decided on the hug after all, giving her a little kiss to the forehead to go with it as I assured her, "Kenn, you just gotta chill. This shit is... it's messy as hell. And trust me, I know the feeling. But it'll all work itself out. Don't worry."

She finally smiled, nodding her head as if she actually believed me.

"Now, to answer your question, the only alcohol I have are those little *Lime-A-Rita* things. But I bet you're too classy for those, huh?"

She brushed me off. "Not in the slightest. It only takes two to get a nice buzz."

I couldn't help but laugh as I told her, "Kennedy,

you can't go bowling drunk. Your ass is gonna fuck around and go sliding down the lane."

"If I'm lucky, I'll hit my head on the pins hard enough to get a concussion so I can forget any of this ever happened."

I was just getting ready to scold her for talking crazy when Miles jogged down the stairs. Once he saw it was Kennedy who had shown up, he tossed out, "Sup, sis?"

"*Sis*?" Kennedy and I asked simultaneously.

He looked between the two of us with a goofy smile before continuing his original quest towards the kitchen without answering. And even though I pretended to be just as confused as Kennedy was, I knew exactly what Miles was implying.

"Yesssss, Chloe! That's my friend, y'all!"

Miles and Wes snickered at Kennedy's clearly drunken celebration for her friend's strike to win the game while I could only sit back and smile. I told her not to get drunk, but her hardheaded ass insisted on taking a third *Lime-A-Rita* to-go.

Now she was most definitely feeling the buzz.

Kennedy and Chloe smacked hands before they headed back to the sitting area. She literally fell into my lap, wrapping an arm around my neck as she yelled to the group, "It's official. We're going pro."

Now I couldn't help but laugh as I busted her bubble. "Kennedy, Chloe did all the work. You just cleaned up a few lucky shots."

She put a hand to her ear, looking around as she said, "Y'all hear that? I heard a... *hater*!"

Everybody laughed again as I gave her a little kiss to the cheek. She turned to me with a grin of her own as she landed a peck on my nose.

"Oh my God. How cute are y'all?!" Chloe gushed.

I couldn't answer as I was too wrapped up in Kennedy's eyes while they bore into mine. She put a hand to my face, scrubbing a hand over my beard as she said, "I always knew you were trouble."

I wrapped my arm around her waist, securing her position to tell her, "I could say the same about you, baby."

Chloe attempted to intervene once more. "Seriously?! I can't even take this overload of cuteness right now!"

Kennedy smiled, leaning in for a kiss until Miles yelled, "Get a room!"

I turned my head away from Kennedy's lips as she began to giggle. "Damn, little bro. Quit hatin'."

"I'm not hatin', though this fifth wheel role is *definitely* some bullshit."

Wes reached over to smack him on the back of the head as he said, "You won't be saying that when you're down in Atlanta in a couple days knockin' boots with Ava."

He looked proud as he responded, "You damn right! And I can't wait. Matter of fact, carry on, y'all. I'ma go to the bathroom and *FaceTime* her now. You know, build up the anticipation."

We all expressed our disgust as we watched him take off.

I looked across the table at Wes who immediately went into conversation with Chloe, then I looked at Kennedy who was all smiles as she gazed into space.

I pushed her hair behind her ear as I asked, "What's on your mind, Kenn?"

She snapped out of it, turning to me to respond, "I don't know. I'm just... this feels good."

165

I couldn't have agreed more, but I decided to up the ante. "Ya know, it can feel even better."

She leaned in a little closer, her forehead pressed against mine. "Oh yeah? How do you suggest we make that happen?"

A million sinful ideas came to my head. But instead of giving away all my secrets, I simply told her, "I can show you better than I can tell you, baby."

Kennedy

"Goodnight, y'all."

I waved a timid goodnight to Miles as he headed up the stairs, leaving Bryson and I alone. And then it settled in. The fact that I was still here - *in his home* - kind of, sort of agreeing to break our two-week agreement even though neither one of us had spoken those exact words.

Nervous was an understatement.

I could feel him staring at me from the opposite couch in his living room as he asked, "So... what you wanna do now? I can find something for us to watch on *Netflix*."

My goofy, still semi-tipsy smile showed up its own. "Bryson, are you tryna *Netflix* and chill me?"

His smile was crooked as he insisted, "Heavy on the chill. But I respect you, Kenn. And I know we made a deal, so..."

"You're right. We did. But that doesn't mean you have to sit a whole room away from me," I replied as I patted the empty space on the couch next to me.

He stroked his beard as if he was considering taking me up on the offer. "Actually, it does. Cause if I come over there, I'm breaking the hell out of our deal."

Now we're talkin'...

"Who says I'm gonna let you?" I teased.

He took a deep breath, looking borderline upset as he said, "Kennedy... don't do that."

"Don't do what?"

"Don't even engage in this conversation with me.

Shit, it's hard enough to have you in my house after hours lookin' as sexy as you do. And you've been teasing me all night like I actually had a shot. But I know you're kinda... emotional right now, whether you believe it or not. And I don't want it to seem like I'm taking advantage of you by being the first to..."

I cut him off. "Bryson, will you just shut up and get your ass over here already?"

"*Kennedy...*"

"Just listen to me, Bryson. *Please.*"

He scrubbed a hand down his face as if he just knew it was a bad idea before he finally stood up and made his way to my couch, settling a respectable distance away.

"Bryson, are you serious right now?"

He wouldn't even look at me to answer, "Very."

I turned to him, my knee bent on the couch as I asked, "What happened to all that stuff you were talking at the bowling alley?"

"You were on my lap, Kenn. That kind of closeness brings out the demons."

In one swift move, I was straddling his lap, grabbing his hands and placing them on my waist. "Well... now what?"

He breathed my name onto my lips, "*Kennedy...*"

I was way too eager and anxious as I answered, "Yes, Bryson?"

He looked me dead in my eyes as if he was checking my pupils. "You sure about this? You're not still drunk, are you? Scale one to ten..."

I thought it over and quickly came up with an answer. "Umm... five. Strong five. On the scale. Grown as hell. *Bars....*"

He busted out laughing at my impromptu freestyle, almost causing us to bump heads. Then he wore the sexiest smirk as he confessed, "Kennedy, you're gonna fuck around and make me fall in love with your ass."

My heart fluttered as I wrapped my arms around his neck, letting my forehead fall to his before I teased, "Oh, you mean you aren't already? If I were you, I'm pretty sure I would be."

He gave me a quick kiss before he replied, "Nah. Before I do that, I have to do a final test."

I snuck a kiss of my own, then a second before I asked, "Oh yeah? What's that?"

"Gotta see what that pussy talkin' 'bout."

"Oh my God!" I screeched with a laugh as he took control of the situation, standing up and forcing me to wrap my legs around his waist. I held on tight as he latched his hands under my thighs and carried me up the stairs.

"You gotta be quiet, baby. Unless you're tryna get caught by Miles. I'm sure he's waiting with an ear against his door," he whispered as I inhaled the faint smell of his cologne against his neck.

He kicked open the door to his master bedroom, then used his back to shut it as I replied, "He's in college, Bryson. I'm sure he's heard much worse."

That stopped him dead in his tracks.

"Kennedy, you must not know what you're getting yourself into right now. He's never heard *anything* like this. You've never *felt* anything like this."

I shuddered from just the thought. Surely he couldn't be all talk.

I smiled as he carried me over to the bed, laying me down gently before pulling his shirt over his head. The little hint of moonlight gave just enough of a glow for me to see his perfectly tattooed-chest, though it certainly wasn't the first time.

But now…

Now it was different.

He was different.

And I was… *available.*

He worked to get out of his jeans as he expressed, "Baby, you have on *way* too many clothes right now. Get comfortable. I'll be right back." Then he disappeared into the master bathroom.

Hmmm… What's comfortable?

Bra and panties?

Just panties?

Nothing at all?

He was already back, carrying what looked like a bottle of lotion by the time I came to a decision.

He looked confused to see me still in all of my clothes, prompting him to ask, "Kenn, are you having second thoughts?"

"No! I mean… *no.* I'm just… in my own head. I'm good. I promise."

He smiled, setting the bottle on his nightstand before he offered, "Here. Let me help you." Then he crawled onto the bed, hovering over my bottom half to unbutton my jeans before tugging them down my thighs.

"Comfy?"

"Umm… almost."

He rose an eyebrow before he climbed higher, and I lifted just enough for him to pull my shirt over my head.

"*Damn, Kenn.*"

I instantly became concerned. "What? What's the matter?"

He chuckled, licking his lips as he answered, "Nothing. Nothing at all. You're just… sexy as fuck."

I blushed instantly. "Thank you, Bryson."

"Don't thank me yet. Roll over on your stomach."

I wasn't sure what he had in mind, but I did as he asked, stuffing my face into the pillows that were permeated with his lingering scent. I felt him unsnap my bra, and soon after his hands, covered in a warm liquid, were gently kneading my back. I groaned, sinking deeper into the mattress.

He worked my back, moving up to my shoulders and neck before moving down to my legs. Then he pulled my panties just slightly as he asked, "May I?"

Instead of answering, I lifted my lower half just enough so that he could remove them. He started on my calves first, then moved to my feet for a short stint before going back up to my thighs.

I could feel the motions of his fingers getting a little more intricate as he slightly grazed between them, teasing me by not quite touching me where I was desperate to feel him. And when he finally did brush against my swollen flesh, I almost exploded.

I could hear the amusement in his voice as he asked, "Hmmm… you like that, baby?"

I nodded ferociously, my hair becoming an instant mess. I heard him shifting in the bed behind me before I felt his lips against my bare back.

"Kennedy, you drive me crazy. I mean… how is it even possible for you to be this damn perfect? Smart… and sexy. Innocent… and yet, still a damn mystery." He capitalized each of his compliments with kisses along my spine. I was just sure my back was going to engulf in flames.

He finally made his way to my neck, stopping to whisper in my ear, "Kennedy, are you on birth control?"

I turned my head, peeking back to answer, "Like clockwork."

"Can I… feel you? All the way?"

My toes curled as he tugged my ear between his teeth.I could hardly think straight, but managed to attempt a response, "Bryson, I…

He cut me off, moaning in my ear, "Kennedy,

please. I've… I've never done it with anyone else. I want you to be the first. I want… *you* to be the only."

All types of shit ran through my head, but none of it stopped the breathy, *"Okay"* I released just before he slid inside of me; so slowly, so deeply, so fully that I wanted to scream.

So I did.

He let out a sexy little chuckle right against my ear, not stopping to say, "Baby, you gotta be quiet, remember?" His words sounded foreign as I focused on what he was doing to my body.

My body.

Oh my God, it would never be the same.

We would never be the same.

But as I continued to enjoy the feel of his every move, that suddenly became the least of my worries.

Bryson

I'm gonna marry this damn girl.

That's the kind of crazy, psycho shit that was running through my head as I watched Kennedy sleep, her lips in a content little smile as her chest rose up and down.

The night we had shared together was magic. Pure damn magic that only a perfect ass princess like Kennedy could've manifested.

My phone vibrated on the nightstand and I quickly picked it up, not wanting to wake Kennedy up. But once I saw it was Leslie, I pressed ignore.

She could wait.

She called back a few more times and I ignored them all, too busy watching Kennedy as she stirred a little then readjusted against the pillows with her eyes shut. My phone chimed to signal I had a text, and since I knew that wouldn't disturb Kennedy, I opened the message.

Boss Lady Les: URGENT! URGENT! CALL ME ASAP!

The text was alarming enough to get me out of bed, but of course that woke Kennedy right up. Her eyes were squinty as she asked, "Hey, where you goin'?"

"Leslie called. I'll be right back."

She appeared satisfied with my answer, turning over without a care in the world.

Damn, I could get used to this.

I closed the door and jogged down the stairs as I dialed Leslie's number. There were no pleasantries to her greeting as she asked, "Checking or savings?"

"Huh?"

Her tone was clipped as she explained, "Nicole's $20,000. Is it coming out of your checking or your savings?"

I made my way to the kitchen, grabbing the orange juice from the fridge and a glass from the cabinet as I asked, "What are you talking about, Leslie? I'm not giving her any money."

"Oh, you'll be giving her a lot more than this. Got the DNA test back, and guess what? It *is* yours."

I dropped the glass on the floor, causing it to shatter. *Shit.*

I went to the closet, grabbing a broom as I tried to stay calm when I asked, "What do you mean, it's mine?"

She laid the sarcasm on thick as she answered, "Umm.... let's see. Where should I begin? When a strong, stout sperm cell swims his way through the vagina and finds an egg to connect with, it makes a baby."

"Leslie, that's impossible. I mean, not that... *obviously*. But none of my sperm cells went to her damn vagina," I replied using her language.

"Well *obviously*, it did. I'm looking at the results right now, Bryson."

This just can't be true...

"Man... I gotta see this shit for myself. Email it to me."

"I already did."

I peeked up from my sweeping to find Kennedy wearing a sexy little grin as she strutted over to me in one of my t-shirts.

Damn, I could really *get used to this.*

"*Bryson*? Bryson, you still there?"

My eyes stayed on Kennedy as I told Leslie, "I'll call you back", pressing end even though she was still talking. Then I sat my phone on the counter so I could pull Kennedy into an embrace. She giggled when I grabbed her ass, discovering she wasn't wearing any panties.

"Good morning, Bryson. I borrowed your shirt. I hope you don't mind."

"Hell no, I don't mind. You look way better in it than I ever did. But let's talk about what's *under* this shirt."

She giggled again when I tried to lift it to get a better view of her. "Nu uh. Miles is still here. If you want *that* kind of treatment, you have to come back to bed."

The news from Leslie was immediately erased as I took Kennedy by the hand and led her back up the stairs for a round two.

"Okay, Kennedy. I'll admit it. I'm officially in love with you."

She laughed me off as she fell back against the mattress with the comforter clutched to her chest, though there was hardly any use in hiding considering I had already seen - *and kissed* - every inch of her.

Her skin was glowing, and her smile was bright as she teased, "Tell me again and I might start believing you."

I rolled over on my side, taking a nibble at her bare shoulder. "I can show you better than I can tell you, baby. You know that."

She rolled over to face me, still keeping the comforter clutched as she replied, "Well if I let you show me anymore in the next twenty-four hours, you'll probably pull a muscle. And considering you have a game tonight, we should probably hold off."

"Kennedy, you're still in my bed *and* you're still naked. Basketball is the last thing on my mind right now."

She giggled as she hopped up from the bed, dragging the comforter with her to the bathroom. I laid there in all my naked glory as I really began to consider my own words.

I mean, what was there *not* to love about Kennedy?

And now she was a single woman, so nothing - well, except for the whole baby thing - stood in the way of us really getting together.

I climbed off the bed to follow her, grabbing my discarded boxers on the way, and found she was already in the shower, singing just like she had been when we were out in L.A. Today's song was something about metaphorically being 'gone' and it showing all over her skin.

Maybe that explained the glow.

"Kenn baby, what are you singing?" I yelled so she could hear me over the water.

She yelled back, "Elle Varner. *I Don't Care.*"

I settled in against the counter as I told her, "I like it. Keep singing."

"Bryson..."

I had no problem begging, "Please, baby. For me."

I heard her sigh before she belted lyrics about someone having zealous eyes that she could stare in all day. Lyrics that I was quick to agree with when I interjected, "Me too, baby."

She laughed before she cut off the shower and asked, "Can you hand me a towel, please?"

"Nu uh. Get yo' fine ass out here first. I wanna see you." My dick was already hard just thinking about her beautiful mocha skin dripping wet.

"Bryson, quit playin'."

176

Though initially I was dead ass serious, I decided to play a little bit. "I'll give you your towel if you promise to come to my game tonight." I could already see my stat line now, looking more glorious than ever just because she was in attendance.

"Chloe already invited me. Wes gave her tickets."

"Welp... guess you gotta come out naked."

She growled before she pulled the shower curtain back and stepped out one pedicured foot at a time, taking my breath away. Then she strutted over to me, stopping right in front of me before reaching around to snatch her towel from the counter.

"Thanks for nothin', Bryson."

I scrubbed a hand over my beard, admiring her before I teased, "You're welcome for everything, Kennedy."

Kennedy

"Girl… I could get used to this."

I smiled as I looked down to the *Louboutin* pumps Bryson had given me for my birthday. They appeared even prettier as they sat in the arena lighting against the court floor.

"Me too, Chloe. Me…. *too*."

It honestly made me sick how quickly I had become wrapped up in everything Bryson Harris. I should've known having sex with him would take things to unbelievable heights, but I couldn't have predicted the afterglow from just *being* with him as a person, living his lifestyle, taking the role as his…

Chill out, Kennedy.

It was way too easy to get caught up in the fairy tale knowing good and damn well Bryson may have been charming, but he certainly wasn't a prince.

He was a player.

So I couldn't allow myself to get too comfortable, though everything felt *amazing*.

The buzzer went off signaling the beginning of a new quarter and I instinctively clapped my hands as Bryson fixed his shorts before walking to the court. He peeked up at me, giving me a quick smile before he slapped hands with Wes.

"Wes is soooo gonna be my baby daddy. I mean, will you just look at him, Kennedy?! He is soooo fine."

Wes was definitely a looker, but my eyes were on Bryson's frame looking simply divine in his uniform.

"How about your husband, Chloe? Can we do that first before you start poppin' out the man's babies?"

She sighed as we both watched the game go into action.

"Men like Wes don't get married, Kennedy. They make children, they may even get engaged, but they never *really* settle down. So the least I could do is lock-in some child support checks and occasional visits."

I almost spit my drink right onto the court.

"Chloe, you can *not* be serious right now. You have a good job. You're a good person. Why in the world would you settle for *child support checks* and *occasional visits*?"

She shrugged, not bothering to answer as she took another sip of her drink. I brushed her off as I turned my attention back to the game just as Bryson was shooting a three-pointer.

All net.

"You're the one who needs to be careful though, Kennedy."

I turned back to her as she wore a goofy little smirk.

"What are you talking about, Chloe?"

"Girl… you're fallin' harder than Alicia Keys. I see the way you keep looking at him, biting your lip and thinkin' 'bout the dick."

I almost got offended as I replied, "I am *not* thinking about his dick. Was it marvelous? *Definitely.* But I'm not sweatin' him like that right now. We're just havin' some fun." I hoped saying it out loud would convince me of it actually being true.

"Yeah, you're havin' some fun alright. The kinda fun that keeps the pussy a tolerable sore."

I smacked her on the arm as she started to laugh.

"But really though, Kennedy. Don't get too attached. Bryson doesn't strike me as the type to be a one-woman

man."

Though I knew she was telling the truth, I also knew I didn't really have control of what was happening between Bryson and I. It was a storm, *a tornado*, taking me with it for the ride, and I could only hope it wouldn't spit me out before it was over.

But of course I couldn't let Chloe know that. So I took another sip of my drink, crossing my legs as I told her, "I got this, Chloe. Trust me. I know what I'm doing."

"So... how'd I do?"

Bryson was on his side, head propped against a bent arm while he used his free hand to draw lazy circles around my belly button.

"That was amazing, Bryson."

He chuckled, moving his hand to my face to stroke my cheek. "I'm not talking about that, baby. I'm talking about my game. How'd I do?"

I tried to sit up a little more, pulling the comforter with me. "*Oh.* You did good. You know that. The reporters were all over you."

He fell to his back, looking at the ceiling as he replied, "That kinda stuff doesn't really matter to me. I want a real opinion from an unbiased eye like yours. So really... how'd I do?"

I thought about the question a little longer before I turned to him the same way he had been looking at me and answered, "Honestly, you're kind of a ball hog. I mean, there were a few times that Wes was wide open and you still took the shot yourself."

His eyes remained on the ceiling, his lips in a closed line as he thought about my impromptu assessment.

From the look on his face, I almost wondered if I had

said too much until he finally piped out, "You're right."

There was no use in hiding my shock from Bryson giving me some credit. "I'm... *right*? I'm actually right?"

He laughed, turning back to his side and pulling me into his arms as he said, "Yes, baby. You're so right. I should've passed the ball more. I'll do better next time; okay?"

I nodded my head against his chest, still a little caught off-guard. "Uh... *yeah.* Yeah okay."

He snuggled me a little closer and we laid together contently, just enjoying the sounds of each other's rhythmic breathing. I knew I had a home of my own, but nothing felt more at home than this exact moment in Bryson's arms.

"Kennedy, can I be honest with you?"

"Please," I whispered, nervous of what he was going to say.

"I love how this feels."

My heart fluttered, but I needed to hear more so I asked, "What do you mean?"

He sighed, kissing the top of my head as he clarified, "*This.* You and I. I don't know what it is, but I *love* this shit."

I nodded my head to agree, unable to actually speak as I already felt a little choked up.

"Are you afraid?"

I swallowed hard so I could ask, "Afraid of what?"

"Afraid of feeling like this."

My heart certainly wasn't throbbing for no reason, so I answered with an honest, "Kinda."

"Me too. I've never felt this before."

I could only respond with a short, "Me neither."

He pulled from under me so that he could see my face, staring down on me as he said, "Kenn, you were engaged. What do you mean, you never felt like this?"

Ugh, where do I begin?

"I'm not really interested in talking about that right now." I hoped he wouldn't press me for answers I didn't really have myself.

He still looked hopeful as he asked, "Maybe one day?"

"If you keep me around long enough to tell you," I teased.

He smiled, leaning in close to hover right over my face and say, "Kennedy, I plan on keeping you around for as long as I'm around."

I closed my eyes, embracing the swoon that enclosed me. I felt his fingers grazing my skin as he said, "Now back to my *amazing* performance…"

"Did I say that? I meant it was… *alright*. Subpar at best."

He laughed as he climbed on top of me, stealing a kiss and then a second.

"Kennedy, you're a freak."

"No I'm not. I just… want the best for you. You know, gotta practice to be perfect."

He parted my legs with his hand, teasing me as he adjusted his own body.

"Well in that case, let me get my ass in this gym ASAP."

Bryson

"You look... *different*."

I fell into my normal chair in front of Leslie's desk as she eyed me skeptically. I had a good feeling of what she was talking about, but I wasn't in the mood to give her any indication of what was really going on; especially with the subject matter of our little impromptu unplanned parenthood meeting in the back of my head.

"What are you talkin' about?"

She stood up, rubbing a hand on her chin as she walked to my side of the desk. I watched her approach until she eventually stood right in front of me and tilted my chin with her hand to get a better look at my face.

She appeared amused as she said, "Oh my God. Ohhhhhh my God."

Naturally I thought something else was wrong, replying with a concerned, "What, Leslie? What is it?"

She took a step back, looking at me with amazement. "You! You're... *in love*. Bryson Harris has fallen in love! Well I'll be damned."

I brushed her off. "Leslie, quit playin'. I'm not in love."

Apparently I wasn't convincing enough as she asked, "Who is she? You make amends with your baby mama or somethin'?"

The title alone grinded my gears. I mean, what was somebody like me supposed to do with a damn baby mama?

It can't be true.

"I don't have one of those."

She brushed me off the same way I had done her, waving a hand as she said, "Right. Still holding onto the innocence. I get it. But really, somebody's got your nose wide open. So who is it?"

I thought it over quickly, knowing there was no use in trying to hide it from Leslie. She found out everything eventually.

"Ah... *shit*. It's Kennedy."

Her face went from amused to confused. "*Kennedy*? Like... ex-stylist Kennedy? *Engaged* Kennedy? Gotdamnit, Bryson. I told you to leave that girl alone."

I quickly explained, "She's not engaged anymore. And she's been... staying with me for the last couple of days. And I... I don't know what I'm doing, Leslie. But everything feels so damn good."

It was scary how quickly I had become consumed by everything Kennedy Wilson, but I honestly shouldn't have been surprised considering how much she had been on my mind even when we weren't involved.

"So you really are in love?"

I put my head in my hands before I nodded yes.

"Wow. Never thought I'd see the day."

I peeked up at her, visibly exhausted by the conversation because I knew there was way more than I was leading on. And of course Leslie picked up on it.

"Wait a minute... what's the problem? You should be happier than this."

I tossed my hood on to cover my eyes before I leaned further back in the chair.

"She umm... I haven't told her yet. About the baby."

"Well why not?"

There were a couple of reasons I hadn't brought it up yet, including how much of our time was spent doing more talking with our bodies than anything. But I was sure Leslie didn't care much about that part of it, so I told her, "Well for one, I'm still in disbelief. For two, I don't know how she's gonna take it. I'm scared of what her reaction may be."

Leslie went back to her chair, putting her elbows on the desk as she reasoned through it. "You don't wanna lose her already. I get it. But you have to tell her, Bryson. I mean, it's either you tell her or she finds out in the streets, and that'll make shit a lot worse for you."

I hate it when she's right...

"Yeah I know. I just don't have it in me to do something so risky quite yet." The last thing I wanted to do was hurt Kennedy in her still pretty vulnerable state.

Leslie let out a laugh as if she thought what I had said was ridiculous. "*Risky*? Do we really wanna talk about *risky*? You had sex with a woman on the first night, got her pregnant, and you're second-guessing being *risky*? You truly amaze me, Bryson."

"We still have to wait for that later round of DNA tests, Leslie. But sex is... simple, easy. Losing Kennedy would break me."

She looked almost as exhausted as me when she replied, "Well Bryson, if you really feel that strongly about her, then she deserves to know the truth. From you. So handle it."

It was easier said than done, but Leslie was right. Kennedy deserved the truth.

So I would just have to suck it up and give it to her.

"Bryson, what's the matter?"

Damn, quit lookin' so suspicious.

I took a slow sip of my wine, trying to figure out why people liked this shit so much before I looked across the dinner table at Kennedy and told her, "Nothing's the matter, baby." I almost choked just saying the word *baby* out loud, thinking Kennedy may pick up on where the conversation was heading.

She eyed me suspiciously, similar to the way that Leslie had done in her office earlier in the day.

"Something is definitely wrong. It's the finals and you're drinking. Wine at that. So just tell me. Is it something with the team?"

I shook my head no.

"Is it something I said? Something I did? You tired of playing house with me already?" she teased.

I quickly assured her, "Hell no, Kenn. I'm actually gettin' ready to lock you in here and throw away the key."

She giggled, taking a sip of her wine before she continued pressing, "But seriously. You've been acting strange ever since that meeting with Leslie. She finally kicking you to the curb as a client?"

That one I could definitely brush off. "She wouldn't dare. She knows I'm her cash cow."

She rolled her eyes as she rattled, "Forever the cocky one."

I couldn't help but toss out, "Word on the street is that you like the cocky one quite a bit."

"*Eh...* He's alright."

That little statement, though I knew she was only teasing, got me fired up.

"Oh, just alright? Do I have to remind you how much you like me?"

She shrugged, taking a short sip of her wine and eye-fucking me over the rim of the glass as she answered, "Maybe."

Damn, this girl drives me crazy.

"Kennedy, if you're hungry you better eat now cause

I'm not gonna be able to hold off on touching you for much longer."

I wasn't really sure how I had lasted this long, but I suppose the bit of news I needed to share helped me to keep my distance.

She took another sexy sip of wine before she groaned, "The only thing I'm *hungry* for is you."

That shit was like music to my ears.

I pushed out of my seat and walked over to hers as she stood up to meet me.

"Kennedy, I love you."

Instead of telling me back like I expected, she challenged me, "Hmph... prove it."

I wrapped an arm around her waist, pulling her close enough to whisper in her ear, "My pleasure."

One more day, Bryson.

Just one more day.

Kennedy

Everything felt so perfect.
Sexy and beautiful.
Sinful but blissful.
Secure, and yet still… *free*.

Bryson's arm was draped across my waist as he spooned me. Though according to his morning wood, he'd be forking me at any given moment. And I'd devour it, because every single time with Bryson felt just as exciting as the first.

I was gone.

So far gone, in so deep, that it honestly scared the crap out of me. But I suppose a little bit of that carefree, go with the flow energy Bryson loved to apply to life was starting to rub off on me. He had even confessed his love for me on more than one occasion, and though I wasn't quite ready to say it back, I was grateful to know I wasn't alone in my feelings.

My phone vibrated against the nightstand. But when I reached to get it, Bryson's hold on my waist got tighter.

"Nu uh, baby. I'm not lettin' you run away from me yet."

I giggled as I tugged a little harder and told him, "I'm just grabbing my phone, Bryson."

He gave me just enough slack to grab it before he pulled me back in even closer than I had been before.

He was already peppering kisses against my bare shoulder as I opened the text from Chloe.

Chloe Cartrashian: Girl… did you know Bryson

has a baby on the way?!?

I pulled away from him just enough to reply without him being able to see the screen.

Kenn'dall: Yeah. He told me it's not his, though.

I didn't feel it was necessary to mention my still-suspect conversation with the culprit herself.

Chloe Cartrashian: So you already saw this?...
link

I clicked the link and the header alone made my heart skip a beat.

Baller Bae turned Baby Daddy

So we should've known it was only a matter of time before our favorite baller bae, Bryson Harris, got trapped by a member of the groupie gang. But it's been confirmed that he has a child on the way with none other than Nicole Cooper (@nikkicoop on Instagram for the creepers who just have to see what she looks like). She's cute, so we're sure the baby will be too. But we're still not happy to see one of our favorites go. Check out a gallery of our favorite pics of Bryson from over the years below!

I read the little blurb twice to make sure I hadn't missed anything, but there it was in fine print.

Confirmed.

No longer slim chance, but *confirmed*.

And he knew.

He *had* to know.

I removed his arm from around my waist and went straight for my clothes that were scattered all over the room.

"Kenn baby, what's the matter?"

The tears were already forming as I snatched my pants from the floor. "You... you *knew*."

He sat up concerned, tossing his long legs to the edge of the bed so that he could stand up and ask, "I knew what, baby?"

"The baby. It's yours. It's really yours. And you knew! When the fuck were you gonna tell me, Bryson? *Huh*? Were you gonna fuck me a few more times and toss it in as a *by-the-way* over pillow talk? Send me a cute little text with it tagged on the end? Leave a note on the fuckin' fridge?!" The tears gushed out of hiding in no time at all.

I was pulling my shirt down over my head as he pleaded, "Baby, please calm down. I was gonna tell you last night, but then..."

"But then nothin'! I don't wanna hear it, Bryson! Have a fuckin' fantastic life with your fuckin' fantastic family!"

Just the thought of Bryson with someone else made me want to throw up.

He remained calm, following me down the stairs as he explained, "Kennedy, Nicole and I will never be a family. We made a common mistake as grownups and now we have to deal with it. But that was well before you and I became a thing."

I stuffed my feet into my shoes that were thankfully waiting for me at the door as I replied, "I knew that coming into this, Bryson. But you *knew*... and you held it from me. I've been with you every damn day and you *held* it from me. How am I supposed to feel about that?"

I felt pathetic as I wiped away the tears that were steadily streaming down my face. He attempted to pull me into a hug, but I pushed him away.

"Kennedy, I'm sorry. I swear I was gonna tell you."

"Kinda like how you were gonna tell me about the damn baby in the first place? *Right*. I'm out of here. Just... do me a favor and leave me the hell alone."

I yanked open the door, but he stopped it from opening completely with a stiff arm.

"I can't do that, Kenn. I love you too much for that shit. Don't let this pull us apart, baby."

I almost believed him until I remembered who I was dealing with. Sure he had been sweet as of late, but he was still Bryson.

Same ol' player ass Bryson.

So I faced him straight up, feeling bolder than ever before as I told him, "You're really good at this. Your whole, *'I fucked up but keep me around anyway'* spiel is like... A1. *Rehearsed.* Practiced to be made perfect which tells me everything I need to know about you. So like I said, leave. me. the hell. *alone!*"

I took the long way home, which really did nothing but allow me to cry in the comfort of my car for way longer than I should've been. I mean, where were these tears coming from anyway? Why was I so emotional about this fool?

Because you love him, Kennedy.

That's why.

"Well love sucks!" I answered myself out loud as I pulled into the parking lot of my apartment complex. It took me a few minutes to pull myself together before I walked inside, surprised to see all of the lights on.

What the hell?

I could hear singing coming from the shower, and since I knew it wasn't me, I could only attribute the lyrics to one person.

Landon.

Why is he still around?

Better question... how long has he been around?

I quietly walked to the bathroom, opening the door to only be hit with a burst of steam. I made my way further inside, flushing the toilet so *he* would get hit with freezing cold water.

"Shit! What the!" He pulled back the shower curtain and I just stood there with my arms crossed and a scowl on my face.

"Why are you here?"

He shrugged before reaching back to turn the water off. "Hotels got too expensive. So I came back since you haven't been here in who knows how long."

I rolled my eyes, thinking about where I had been spending all of my time before I told him, "Well I'm back now. So you need to get out of here."

He stepped out, wrapping a towel around his waist as he challenged me, "I don't technically have to leave, Kennedy. I had already paid my share of the rent for the month before all this shit went down. So unless you plan on coughing up a prorated refund, I'll be here for a little while."

Since I was technically unemployed, I knew that wasn't even possible.

"Fine, Landon! Just stay out of my way, alright?"

He laughed, rubbing his lotion in as he said, "Shit was too good to be true, huh? You should've known that before you invested so much in him, Kennedy. You knew who you were dealin' with."

I was far more annoyed than I could handle.

"Fuck you, Landon. How about *you* deal with that?"

He laughed again and I stormed out of the bathroom, heading straight to the bedroom and slamming the door behind me. Then I closed every last blind, stripped out of my clothes, and crawled into bed for good.

Bryson

I didn't want to go.

It was the final game of the series, the game that would decide if we were league champions for the second time in three years or if we were runner-up for the second time in three years. Losing last year's game had been a pretty tough pill to swallow, but nothing felt as tough as dealing with Kennedy leaving me. My chest felt heavy, my head felt light, and *I was…* I was so lost that even simple tasks like taking a shower felt like moving mountains.

My phone had been ringing off the hook ever since that stupid ass article dropped, but I only answered the ones from Miles, Wes, and Leslie. Miles was pissed at me for not telling him about his "nephew", Wes was wondering why I was running so late for shootaround, and Leslie was keeping me up-to-date on my PR Rep's moves to get this whole thing squashed. They still couldn't pinpoint if Nicole had broken our non-disclosure agreement or if it was someone else who had dropped the news, but none of that seemed as important as figuring out how to get Kennedy back.

Seeing her cry - *making her cry* - literally broke my heart. It wasn't the first time a girl had cried over me to my face, but something about Kennedy's tears felt like bullets to my chest.

I had fucked up.

Fucked up her trust in me, fucked up our vibes, fucked up our energy.

And *that*, I couldn't live with.

I should've been heading to the arena, but instead I got dressed and headed straight to Kennedy's apartment. It took a few knocks before the door was answered, and once it was, my heart fell to my feet.

Landon was wearing the smuggest look as he said, "Can I help you with something?"

"Where's Kennedy?" I had already saw her car in the parking lot, so I knew she was home.

"I don't think she's really interested in the likes of you right now, bruh. But don't worry, I'm taking *good* care of her."

I bit the inside of my cheek, clenching my fists tight as I tried to stop myself from throwing a punch. I was sure a reaction was all he really wanted.

I rubbed the back of my neck to self-soothe as I said, "Just umm... tell her I stopped by, alright?"

He shrugged before he replied, "Maybe I will. Maybe I won't."

I cocked my head to the side, trying to figure out what Kennedy ever saw in this clown. Surely she wasn't giving him the time of day like he was insisting, but that didn't stop the idea from giving me a headache as I walked back to the car.

The game came and went in a flash.

I could only vaguely remember the champagne-showers in the locker room, and that was simply because I almost got blinded by a cork when I zoned out for the umpteenth time.

None of it felt as good as I imagined it to and I knew it was all because of her. Not that she had done anything wrong, but the fact that she wasn't there to celebrate with me made it feel less important; less monumental.

I was dazing off again when Wes draped an arm around my shoulder and pulled me in to tease, "MVP! MVP! You were on fire tonight, bro!"

It was crazy that my recollection of the game wasn't good enough to determine if he was right.

"Thanks, man."

He let me go and I continued down the hall to the postgame interview room. But once I realized he wasn't walking with me, I turned around and found him with a confused look on his face.

"What's up, bro? Aren't you comin'?"

He took the few steps over to where I stood, taking a closer look at me before he said, "Yeah. I was just tryna figure out what the hell is wrong with you. We just won a championship, B. A championship! And looking at you, you would've thought we got our asses kicked."

Damn, is it that obvious?

I did my best to convince him otherwise, forcing a smile as I told him, "I'm good, bro. Don't trip."

He only sighed before he replied, "You ain't gotta fake it, B. Chloe already told me what happened with you and Kennedy."

Damnit.

I tried to brush him off as best as I could. "Nah, I'm not even trippin' off that. It is what it is. I'm just ready to get these interviews over with so I can roll to the crib."

I wanted nothing more than to grab one of the leftover *Lime-A-Rita's*, take a long bath, and get in bed. But of course, Wes looked at me like I had said the most ludicrous thing he'd ever heard.

"*The crib*? You can *not* be serious right now. We gotta go out and celebrate, man. You know that."

I continued my pursuit of the interview room and he followed closely.

"I think I'ma sit this one out, Wes. Not really in the mood to party."

He walked next to me stride for stride as he asked, "Damn. She really fucked your head up, didn't she?"

"If it was only my head, I wouldn't have a problem. It's my heart that's the fucked up one."

The feeling was so foreign, yet so deep. Moms had always told me that once the heart knew, it just knew.

And I definitely knew.

Even more so now, for all the wrong reasons.

Wes looked almost as exhausted as I felt when he said, "Shit, B. You gotta get that back then. Once the heart is involved, it'll never just blow over. No matter what you do, no matter who you screw, she'll always be in the back of your head. You're just gonna have to fight for her forgiveness. If she feels the same way about you, she'll forgive you eventually."

He made it sound so easy, but I knew that was hardly the case when it came to someone like stubborn ass Kennedy.

"I don't have time for eventually. I need her back now." Though it wasn't like that much time had passed since the day she stormed out of my house, it had certainly gone by in slow motion, teasing me for my wrongdoings with every second that ticked away.

We stood outside of the door as Wes put a hand to his chin and said, "Well... I got an idea for how we can expedite the process a little bit."

I could hardly imagine what kind of bullshit Wes had come up with in that head of his. But I really wasn't in a position to turn down any advice, so I told him, "I'll take whatever you're dishin' out, bro."

He pulled me in, whispering his master plan in my ear. And though I knew it was a stretch, it was the best shot I'd have at getting my girl back.

Kennedy

I wasn't sure how much time had passed.

Hell, I really didn't even know what day it was if we were being completely honest.

Nothing other than going to the bathroom felt worthy of getting up for, and thankfully that was only a few steps away.

My stomach felt empty, but I didn't have a taste for anything.

My mouth was dry, but nothing sounded like it would quench my thirst.

My hair was a mess, my skin felt dewy, and I was pretty sure the sleep-lines on my face were a nap away from being permanent.

Long story short, I was a wreck.

And it was all his fault.

I mean… was telling me the baby was actually his really that hard of a task? All it took were a couple of words, and I would've at least been in a position to make the decision of if I was comfortable with the idea or not.

Of course I knew it was always a possibility, and I suppose it was somewhat my fault for not sticking to our original deal. And now that I had developed such strong feelings for him - *had fallen in love with him* - I may have actually considered the arrangement if he would've just told me. But finding out from a friend when the owner of the news had been right next to me – or, inside of me if we're being technical - that was like trying to swallow a horse pill with a swollen throat.

It just wasn't going to happen.

I heard a soft knock on the door, but I really wasn't in the mood to deal with the only person who could be on the other end; Landon. He had checked in on me a few times, and though I was grateful for the teeny ounce of human interaction, he was still in second place on my shit list.

He knocked once more before coming inside, and my nose was instantly assaulted with the smell of greasy cheeseburgers and fresh out of the fryer French fries.

Naturally my stomach growled in response.

He walked over to the blinds, pulling the string to open them and letting in the little bit of light from the night's sky. Then he found a spot on the edge of the bed where I was laying.

He stroked my hair out of my face, wearing the biggest smile as he sat the bag right in front of me.

"Hey babe, you should probably try to eat something. I know you have got to be hungry by now."

"What do you have?"

In a couple of sniffs, I probably could've figured out the exact order. But that was going to require more energy that I had to give.

"Your favorite. Double cheeseburger, add bacon, extra mustard, hold the tomato. And a side of curly fries."

I used the last of my energy to sit up and rip the bag open.

"Damn, girl. You know there's been food in the house all this time."

I rolled my eyes, pulling back the wrapper of the heavenly goodness. Then I lifted the burger to my mouth, completely unbothered by the grease that dripped down to my wrist when I took a bite and moaned as I chewed.

I could feel Landon watching my every move as I took a second bite. Through chews, I managed to ask,

"Why are you looking at me like that?"

He smiled again as he answered, "Because even in this state of... disarray, you're still pretty damn attractive."

I couldn't smile back, but I was able to give a little smirk.

"Well thank you. And thanks for the food."

He nodded as he stood up from the bed. "Anytime, babe. There's a soda too, but I figured you'd prefer a glass of wine."

"*Glass*? More like *bottle*."

He laughed his way out of the door before eventually returning with the bottle and a corkscrew.

"If you need anything else just give me a holler, alright?"

I pulled my hair behind my ear, focusing my attention back on what was left of the burger as I nodded my head yes. And once he was out of sight, all I could think about was how nice he was being to me.

Of course we would never be what we once were, but it still felt good to have someone on my side.

Turning on my phone was a huge mistake.

My head was still fuzzy from drinking half a bottle of wine the night before, so the light alone was irritating. But the endless notifications pouring in took irritation to a whole new level.

Texts from Chloe, texts from Bryson, texts from numbers I didn't even have saved. And then voicemail, after voicemail, after voicemail of... *apologies.*

I couldn't deal.

I replied to Chloe's texts to let her know I was indeed alive and had no intentions of going out anytime soon like she was insisting, then I replied with a capital FUCK YOU to Bryson that never actually got sent.

I scrolled through a few of the texts from numbers I didn't recognize, mostly bloggers looking for information on Bryson, before I found one from someone I actually knew.

Hey sis. I hope all is well. I know you're upset with Bryson, but he really wants to know if you're at least okay. Text me back and let me know if you don't wanna talk to him directly. - Miles

What a sweetheart.

Hey Miles. I'm good. Thanks for checking in on me. Much <3 - KW

Since the text was actually from a few hours earlier, I wasn't expecting a reply. So I was surprised when one did, in fact, come in.

Glad to hear that, ma. And keep being mad at him. He deserves it. ;) - Miles

A real smile crept to my face for the first time in however long I had been holed up in my bedroom. I left my phone on the charger, heading to the bathroom to at least do the bare minimum of taking a shower and brushing my teeth. Then I threw on a clean pair of pajamas and went into the living room to find Landon sound asleep on a makeshift pallet in the middle of the floor with the TV still on from the night before.

To no surprise at all, it was turned to *ESPN*.

I couldn't help but tune in as they went on and on about how Bryson had played lights out for his team to win the championship. I honestly wanted to be happy for him - *wanted to be proud of him* -, but my stubborn side wouldn't allow it. Surely he was celebrating, living in the glory of yet another championship while I hung out around the house beyond miserable.

I couldn't go out like that.

I headed back to the bedroom, put together the best outfit I could find, and spent the next couple of hours getting completely dolled up, from my hair to my makeup and everything in between. Then I grabbed my phone and sent Chloe a text reneging on my initial rejection of her plans.

If he could move on with his life, then so could I.

Bryson

I sure hope his plan works.

I was honestly nervous as I sat at the private bar in the club, wearing all black so that I wouldn't stand out too much even though we were obviously in VIP. But I knew if Kennedy saw me, she would more than likely turn around and get away before I could talk to her. I was surprised when Chloe told Wes she had actually agreed to come out, though I was sure Chloe hadn't given her every detail of what she was really getting herself into.

My back was turned to the crowd when I heard Chloe yell, "There's my superstar!"

My heart started beating even faster just from knowingly being in the same vicinity as Kennedy. I turned around slowly, and my jaw literally dropped to the floor.

She looked flawless as fuck.

Her hair was laid in soft waves that fell perfectly around her face, her makeup looked like she had found all the right tutorials on *YouTube*, and her outfit fit in all the right places giving the classy yet sexy vibe she always pulled off so well.

I could tell she was second guessing her attendance as she watched Chloe throw herself at Wes, but eventually Wes snuck a hug from Kennedy also.

And now it was go time.

I stood up, taking the last sip of my club soda before I headed their way. She didn't see my approach as she was already engaged in a conversation with Wes and

Chloe, so I gently tapped her on the shoulder to get her attention.

When she turned around, she wasn't quite smiling, but she wasn't frowning either. So I felt a little hopeful as I said, "Hi."

"Hello."

We stood there in a fog of silence, neither of us really knowing what to say. Of course I had rehearsed this exact moment a million times before I came, but I guess her beauty threw all that shit out of the window.

I cleared my throat to ask, "Do you think we could umm... go talk?"

She crossed her arms, wearing a hint of a smirk as she asked, "Here?"

I tried to stay calm as I told her, "Yeah. They have a rooftop that's a lot quieter than this. If that's cool with you." I knew if she didn't want to talk to me, there was really no way I could make her.

"Yeah, it's cool with her!" Chloe jumped in, damn near pushing Kennedy into my arms. Kennedy shot her a glare before she took a deep breath and followed me up the stairs to the rooftop.

The setting was a little more intimate than I imagined, with only a few people occupying the lounge-style seating around various pit fires. I wanted to take her hand and guide her to the one I thought would be the most private, but instead I kept my hands to myself and just walked to an unoccupied area.

She fell into her seat, gazing out into the night sky, and I honestly could've just stared at her all-night long. But I knew that wasn't what I had brought her up here for, so I decided to kick up a conversation.

Of course, the second I opened my mouth to say something, she spoke up. "So... I heard you guys won the big game. Congratulations."

"Yeah, thanks."

The silence returned, and it took everything in me not to reach out and touch her. I mean, she looked so damn good that I just knew even the slightest graze of her skin would probably ignite the flame that was brewing inside of me.

I watched her closely as she twiddled with her fingers before she finally turned her attention to me and said, "I umm... guess we should talk, as adults, so we can come to some type of closure... *as adults.*"

"Kenn, I'ma be real with you. I'm not really interested in closure. I'm interested in hashing this shit out so we can move on... *together.*"

She caught the cutest little attitude as she replied, "Well *I'm* not really interested in being with you right now, so it looks like we have a problem."

I could no longer resist the urge to take her hands in mine.

"Baby, come on now. Did I fuck up? *Yes.* Could I have told you right away? *Yes.* But I didn't purposely keep it from you to be malicious."

She didn't pull her hands away, but her little attitude remained as she asked, "Well what do you call it, huh? Protecting my feelings?"

I nodded. "Yes. Exactly that."

She leaned in, dropping her tone to a whisper as she said, "Well guess what, Bryson? You fucked that up regardless."

"*Baby...*"

She finally pulled her hands back into her own lap and released a sigh of her own. I could tell she was just as exhausted with the conversation as I was when she said, "Just tell me, Bryson. Why didn't you tell me right away?"

I gave her the honest truth. "I just... we were in such

———

209

a good place and I didn't wanna ruin it yet. I didn't wanna lose you, Kennedy. And yes, that happened regardless too. But I swear I was gonna tell you when the time was right."

She rolled her eyes as she replied, "There's never a right time to tell someone you love that you're having a baby by someone else."

"See. So now you know where I was coming from."

I was trying to lighten the mood, but she didn't take the bait. Instead she pushed her hair behind her ear, almost appearing too calm to be true as she said, "Look, Bryson. I appreciate everything you did for me, and I respect your position on the situation, but we just... *can't.*"

"Why can't we, Kenn? We were good before this happened. Damn near perfect if we're being real. And I know you love me just as much as I love you. So why can't you look past this one thing?"

Clearly I must've asked the wrong question as she stood up in a fury. "It's not just this one thing!"

A few sets of eyes shot our way, so she lowered her tone to continue, "It's a whole child we're talking about. A child that you're responsible for until it becomes an adult and hell, even after that. So don't try to sit up here and act like I'm being frivolous over something basic. A child is a big fuckin' deal."

I stood up to meet her eyes, stealing her hands one more time to tell her, "You know what, Kennedy? You're right. And I can't expect you to stop everything you're doing, everything you're building, to join me and my problems."

She refused to keep eye contact with me, dropping her eyes to our feet as she asked, "So what are you saying?"

The breath didn't come easy, but I desperately

210

needed it to reply, "I guess I'm saying... though it pains me to say this... I guess this is really goodbye."

I could tell she was initially shocked, but she quickly brushed it off. "I agree. I mean, it's what's best, right?"

"No, but I get it. It's what's best for you. I don't have a voice in this."

"You had a voice. You just refused to use it."

The silence was deafening, as if everything around us had suddenly disappeared. And in my mind, everything *had* disappeared with my attention being completely stolen by her; as always.

"So this is really it, huh?"

She didn't seem thrilled to answer, "Yeah, I guess so."

We shared a few more moments of just... *looking* at each other before she finally pulled away.

"I'm gonna... go back downstairs."

I knew there was no stopping her, so I gave her a nod and told her I'd be down in a minute. And with every step she took away from me, it felt like she was really stepping on my heart.

———

Kennedy

I should've felt good about this.

In all honesty, I should've been *ecstatic* to finally have the answers I wanted and the closure I thought I needed. But somehow, I felt even more horrible than I had before I left my apartment.

For one, I couldn't believe Chloe's ass had set me up to "run into" Bryson. And for two, I wasn't exactly expecting the conversation between Bryson and I to happen anytime soon; if ever.

But what better time than the present, I suppose.

I dragged myself into the apartment, walking right in on a way too comfortable Landon who was lounging on the couch shirtless, sipping a beer even though it was well past two in the morning.

"Hey. Wasn't sure if you were coming back or not tonight."

"Well… here I am."

He scooted over to one side of the couch before he patted a space for me to sit down. And even though I knew I wasn't interested in his comfort, I walked over and plopped down anyway.

I was working to get my shoes off as he asked, "So, did you have fun tonight?"

I nodded my head yes, though I knew it wasn't true.

"Was… he there?"

My attitude was instant, forcing me to spit out, "That's none of your business, Landon."

He had the nerve to laugh at me as he said, "Damn.

So he was there."

I rolled my eyes, standing up to head to the bathroom, but he pulled me back down to the couch.

"My bad, babe. I was just messin' with you. How about you go change into some comfy clothes, then we can watch a movie together or somethin'."

I stood up again as I told him, "Not interested. I'm going to bed."

"You're going to bed? *Yeah right*. You're way too tense to actually get some sleep."

He could tell I wasn't pleased with his assessment, so he threw in, "Look, I'll sit on the floor or somethin' if that makes you feel better about us spending some time together."

I thought it over and realized a movie may actually be the perfect thing to take my mind off of Bryson, even if I did have to sit through it with Landon of all people.

So instead of turning him down once more, I answered, "Fine. But you better not try anything."

It was late.

Like… *really late*.

Like so late that it was almost time for the sun to come up.

But I felt so content as I laid on the couch with Landon sitting in front of me while we watched *Booty Call* like it was brand new; laughing at all the same parts that were funny in the 90s, though I really had no business watching it back then.

Landon looked content as well, smiling while the light from the action on the TV screen flickered off of his face. He really was a fine specimen of man if you were able to look past his *gigantic* mistake of cheating with those damn strippers.

But I was no better.

I had cheated with someone who was probably on his way to being a modern-day Wilt Chamberlain.

Okay, maybe he's not that bad.

At least I hope not...

Landon must've picked up on my vibes as he turned around and asked, "You okay, babe?"

I tried to look as normal as possible as I replied, "Yeah. I'm fine. Just thinking about some things. I'm good, though. Nothing to worry about."

He wore a halfhearted smile, turning around fully to say, "Kennedy, we were engaged once upon a time. So I pretty much know you like the back of my hand, including when something is wrong with you. So what is it?"

There was no way I was going to talk to my ex-fiancé about my ex-whatever we called ourselves doing. So I stood up, stretching out a little and forcing a yawn. "Nothing, Landon. I'm just… getting tired. I think I'm gonna crash. Thanks for hanging out with me, though."

The smile was now full blown as he replied, "That's what I'm here for, babe. I got your back."

If only you would've done that from the beginning, I wouldn't be in this mess.

I pushed my petty to the side to toss a, "Good night" over my shoulder while I headed to the room. Then I threw myself onto the bed, already trying to figure out how I was going to deal with the coming days.

Chloe had already asked me to go with her to the Championship parade next weekend. And even though I knew just being around Bryson exhausted me, I was still considering attending. It was a big deal for our city to have a championship team once again, so the least I could do was bask in the excitement of all the festivities.

215

At least this time I'd be a little more prepared to see him.

Or would I....

I honestly wasn't sure how I felt about Bryson's truth. I mean, of course I wasn't happy about it, but I also wasn't as upset as I imagined myself to be after the fact.

His intentions were good; it was his execution that was horrible. But was that really a reflection of who Bryson was?

He had been good to me... really, *really* good to me. We were good together.

So why couldn't we move past this one thing?

That one thing is a baby, that's why.

Even though the baby wouldn't be my responsibility, it would always be a part of him. So if I wanted any parts of him, I'd be sharing it with the baby, which also meant I'd be sharing him with Nicole.

And that was some BS.

But would Nicole really be *that* much of an issue?

I mean, I already knew how catty she could get, but I could pretty much assume Bryson would have no problem keeping her in her place.

Damn.

You've got it bad, Kennedy.

I couldn't believe I was really lying in bed thinking up reasons why I should give Bryson another chance when he had already given up and said goodbye.

We had said goodbye.

So anything more would just be a formality.

Or maybe...

Maybe we weren't done.

Maybe there were actually more chapters of our story left to be written.

I picked up my phone with every intention of sending Bryson a sappy ass text, but I put it back down

———

just as quickly.

If I was really going to go into the deep end, I'd at least have to sleep on it first.

Bryson

"Look, Bryson. I know you don't really wanna do this, but I'm not exactly giving you a choice. It's like a rite of passage when someone does something big for our city and you know that, so I really don't know why you're being so hardheaded about it."

Leslie wasn't even looking at me while she went to work on her phone as we rode the elevator together to the floor that the radio station was located. I had been in the studio before and was quite familiar with the host, but I just wasn't in the mood to deal with anybody I didn't absolutely have to. But according to Leslie, this was an absolute have to; especially after she had complained the whole drive over about how she had sat through multiple mediation sessions with my lawyer and Nicole's.

So I shook hands, gave half-hugs, and set up in front of the microphone with my headset on like I was supposed to. I turned to Leslie ready to show her how annoyed I was, but she quickly gave me a thumbs up through the window before I could get the expression off.

"We're going live, people! In three... two..."

DJ Mix'm hopped on the mic, completely in character as he said, "And we're back with a special guest in the house, a champion if you will, Mr. Bryson "MVP" Harris!"

There was a fake round of applause before I got on the mic to say what's up to the listening audience.

"Now Bryson, first we gotta congratulate you and the squad on bringing the championship back to where it belongs here in Philly. But your performance in that final game was out of this world, bro. What got into you?"

"Honestly man, that game is still a blur. People blew my phone up talking about how legendary it was, and I'm like... I don't even remember any of it." I pushed out a laugh and Mix'm did the same.

"That's crazy! I can't even ball like that in full focus and you're out here doing it unconsciously!"

I laughed again, this time a real one.

"So has anything changed since you've became a two-time champion? I'm sure the ladies are showing you mad love."

"You know they are, man. But I only have eyes for one."

I could feel Leslie's eyes burning through the back of my head, so I didn't even bother turning around. Hell, she shouldn't have asked me to do the interview if she didn't expect me to be honest. But apparently that was like music to DJ Mix'm's ears - *literally* - as he lit up to ask, "Oh word? So Mr. MVP has a special lady in his life?"

"I wish. She's not feeling me right now, but I hope she will again someday."

It was crazy that even after saying a pretty clear goodbye, I was still hopeful that Kennedy would somehow make her way back to me.

"Aw man. So our champ is in the doghouse, huh?" He even cued in the fake boo's.

I couldn't help but laugh as I replied, "Yeah, something like that. But if she *is* listening, I still wanna give her a little shoutout. Love you, Kenn baby." Now came the fake awww's.

"You hear him, Kenn baby? The champ loves you. Go ahead and take him back so he can bring us another championship! Matter of fact, we got a song for that."

My headset was instantly filled with New Edition crooning, *Can You Stand The Rain*. I took it off but could still hear the song faintly as it played through the studio.

Since we weren't on air, DJ Mix'm - whose real name was Malik - decided to strike up a normal conversation.

"So what happened with you and your girl, B?"

I scrubbed a hand down my face, giving my beard a tug as I told him, "She umm... it's kind of a long story."

He laughed, moving his mic from in front of his face as he said, "Well condense it to the two minutes we have left of the song."

I sighed, knowing I didn't really want to talk about it but probably needed to so I wouldn't overthink it on my own.

"Basically... I have a child on the way. She knew it was a possibility, we weren't together when it happened. But when it was actually confirmed, she found out from someone else before I could tell her. Of course that made her mad, we fought, she left. Then I saw her after we had already argued about it and we came to the conclusion that it only made sense for us to say goodbye, even though that's not really what I wanted to do."

He looked confused as he asked, "Well then why'd you go for it? Shit, why'd you even suggest it?"

I shrugged. "I guess I just... I couldn't live with her being unhappy over my mistakes." The last thing I wanted to do was make Kennedy bitter.

He nodded to agree with me as he said, "Ahh, yeah I feel you. Well look, let's finish this interview up, then I'll give you some tips on how I've been married for ten years and counting."

Kennedy

"Well... that was cute."

I sat in the passenger seat stunned as I rode to the mall with Chloe. I hardly ever listened to the radio in my own car, preferring my rotation of the same three CDs. But since we were in Chloe's car, I had heard the whole thing.

The whole thing.

I had to keep blinking to fight off the tears.

I tried to play it cool, looking out of the window as I told her, "It was nice."

She quickly brushed me off. "Oh come on now, Kennedy. That was easily the sweetest thing I've heard in like... the last five years. Maybe even ten."

I knew she was right, but I refused to admit it out loud; especially since I had already been thinking about Bryson pretty heavily. It was almost like the interview, even if I had only heard it by chance, was the icing on the cake I was already thinking about baking.

Now I was ready to actually go buy the ingredients.

"So what do I do, Chloe?" I couldn't believe I was asking her of all people for advice.

She whipped into the parking lot as she confidently shared, "If I were you, I'd show up on his doorstep in only a trench coat and those fancy ass shoes he bought you."

I screeched, "Chloe, be for real! What should I do?"

I watched as she engaged in a parking war with another customer, cutting him off to get into the spot before she finally answered, "Honestly, I think you should take him back, Kennedy. I mean, you've been just as miserable, if not more since y'all... would you call it a break-up?"

I nodded. "Something like that."

She made herself busy checking her face in the sun visor mirror. "Well, anyway. Make him work for it, obviously. But hear him out and decide if it's what you want. I'm pretty sure you'll know right away if you can stand the rain," she said with a laugh as she flipped it close.

Even though her advice wasn't the worst I had ever heard from her, I still couldn't help but tease her as we got out of the car. "Chloe, you're really no help."

She slammed her door shut, walking around the front of it to meet me. "*What*? I gave you the best I had. But I know you, and you're gonna do what you wanna do regardless of what I or anyone else tells you. I guess I'm just saving my breath."

I pushed her in the shoulder a little, causing her to stumble away with a laugh.

"But seriously, Kennedy. Just think about it, alright? Give yourself some time... maybe until the parade or somethin', to decide what you wanna do and how you wanna move forward."

In all honesty, it was a really good idea.

A *great* idea.

An idea I could actually make use of.

I pulled my girl in by the arm to tell her, "Thank you, Chloe."

"You're welcome, Kenn. Now since I gave you such stellar advice, I'm gonna need you to put every last one of those stylist skills to use to help me find something cute to wear for Mr. Wes tonight. Gotta keep my champion on his toes."

I couldn't help but laugh as I said, "You've got a deal."

My hands were filled with bags of stuff I really didn't need but still managed to feel good about as I struggled to unlock the front door of my apartment. And for once, Landon's presence paid off as he must've heard me bumping the lock and came to open it.

"Thank you," I tossed out as I slid past him with all of my goods.

"Damn, girl. What'd you do? Buy the whole mall?"

A laugh escaped before I could hold it in. "Shut up, Landon."

I sat the bags down in the bedroom before my nose led me back to the kitchen.

"Mmm… something smells good. What are you cooking?"

He turned around with a smile before he went back to work on the stove. "Some shit one of the other teachers wouldn't stop raving about in our training, so I thought I'd give it a try. Here, how about you come have a taste?"

I thought about turning him down just in case he was trying to poison me or something, but I quickly realized he wasn't *that* damn crazy.

He lifted the spoon, holding his hand under it just in case it spilled, before he brought it to my mouth. I gave him a skeptical eye before I opened my lips and accepted the sample. My skeptical eye shut as I savored the mystery flavor that was the perfect mix of spicy and fruity.

He leaned in, whispering in my ear, "It's good, huh?"

His closeness used to give me tingles, but now it

practically gave me the same reaction as the sauce gave me. Quick burst of goodness that I could pretend to savor before it was, indeed, over.

So I shrugged, stepping away before I told him, "It's alright."

He laughed, turning back to the stove as he said, "Yeah right, Kennedy. I saw that face. It's bomb."

"Well yeah, if that's what you're into. I suppose you'll be... *satisfied.*"

He froze once he digested my words before he went back to stirring. "Well, if you want some of this *non-satisfying* food, it'll be ready in a few minutes."

I was ready to turn him down when my stomach growled, putting me on blast.

Landon laughed as he said, "Mmhm, that's what I thought. You aren't foolin' me."

I really wanted to say something smart back, but there was no use. And besides, a good meal would give me the fuel I needed to figure out my plans with Bryson.

Bryson

"Bro, come on now. You *have* to come to the Championship parade. That shit isn't optional. The whole city will be there."

Wes was pacing back and forth in front of my bed, the bed I had no plans of getting out of just to be around people. Sure I would probably be handed a hefty fine for not attending the parade, probably be deemed the bad guy, and probably lose a bunch of fans, but I honestly didn't care.

She was really gone.

Correction; I had let her go... *willingly.*

And now after talking to DJ Mix'm, I couldn't stop wondering what alternatives we had for handling the situation. Shit, maybe if I would've pleaded my case a little better, we would've had a chance. Or maybe we just needed to go to counseling or something. *Or maybe...*

Wes's voice cut me from my thoughts. "Bryson, are you even listening to me? Look, I know that whole shit with Kennedy still isn't sittin' right, but you've gotta snap out of it. Like ASAP."

I knew he was right, but something made me ask, "Wes, have you ever had your heartbroken?"

He tossed a hand at me like the question was ridiculous. "Hell nah. I don't fall in love. That shit is a trap."

I quickly corrected him, "No. Groupies are a trap. Take it from me."

He nodded his head to agree. "Noted. But for real, B.

We gotta go. Suck that shit up for the people and let's ride out."

I knew he wasn't giving up anytime soon. And even if he did, Leslie would be next to blow up my phone and my doorbell until I showed up.

"Man… alright. I'll be ready in a minute. Wait for me downstairs."

He nodded before he left my room, closing the door behind him. I looked at the Championship shirt he had brought for me to wear. And even though I hardly felt worthy of the title, I pulled it over my head, scrubbing a hand over my hair that was long overdue for a haircut.

Hopefully there's a hat to match the shirt.

I went to the closet to change out of my pajama pants into some jeans and all I could think about was Kennedy sorting through rack after rack until she found the perfect pair for me to wear. She was always so intricate like that, always so on point. I could already imagine her little scowl as I went to pick out a pair of tennis shoes, but I concluded that with this particular event, she wouldn't mind so much.

Damn, I miss that girl.

I went back to the bedroom to grab my phone and shoot her a text. Even if we were done pursuing a relationship, maybe she had actually heard my little spiel on the radio and would consider at least being friends with me again.

Hey Kenn. I wanted to invite you to the Championship parade today at 4 'o clock. I'm pretty sure Chloe's coming too, so you won't be alone or anything, though it's pretty hard to feel alone in a crowd of thousands lol. Let me know. - BS

I finished getting dressed then snatched my phone up to see she had actually replied.

Kennedy: We'll be there.

228

It was so simple, yet it filled me with so much excitement that I could hardly contain myself as I jogged down the stairs to meet Wes.

"Ready, bro?"

He looked at me suspiciously before he asked, "What's gotten into you, man? Just ten minutes ago you were all Danny Downer and shit."

My grin was ear-to-ear as I told him, "She's coming."

He stood up so we could leave but not without asking, "Who?"

I enthusiastically answered, "Kennedy. She's coming to the parade."

He laughed, putting a hand to his forehead as he said. "Aww shit. That's what you're all hyped up about? That girl has got you mad sprung, B."

I knew it was true and there was no denying it. I was crazy about Kennedy, which really only meant one thing.

I had to get her back.

I saw her before she noticed me.

Though most people were cheering us on and trying to catch the different freebies we were tossing out from the float, she was busy on her phone. So instead of calling out to her since I knew she wouldn't hear me, I pulled out my phone and sent her a text.

Look up, Kenn. - B$

I could tell the exact moment she got the text because her head flew up and her eyes locked in on mine before she served up a sugary sweet smile that surprised the hell out of me. I mean, she had actually shown up, so I suppose that was worth something. But I still wasn't expecting her to actually be happy to see me.

While I had her attention, I quickly sent her another text.

Baby, you look absolutely stunning. I miss you so damn much. - B$

She was smiling into her phone, so I took that as a sign to send her one more.

Kennedy, I'm too in love with you to let you go. I'll do whatever it takes to make it up to you, I swear. - B$

I couldn't see her face clearly since our float had passed her, but I could tell she was replying.

Kenn: Whatever it takes, huh?

Whatever it takes, baby. I'll give you the world if I have to. Though, until we get world peace and shit, you should probably hold off on accepting it. - B$

Kenn: LOL. I can't stand you, or the rain, and I swear on that. ;)

Smiling at me.

LOLs.

This had to be a sign for me to make my move.

Well can you stand me enough to let me take you to dinner tonight? - B$

It was risky, but now was a better chance than any to ask her.

It took a little while for a reply to come, but I was more than happy with the results when it did.

Kenn: Sure. Send me the details.

Kennedy

I was nervous. More nervous than I had been for anything in a long time.

Agreeing to going to dinner with Bryson was... not a want, but a need. After sleeping on the whole situation, I had come to the conclusion that I did, in fact, want to be with him. Exactly how we were going to make it work, I wasn't sure. But I was willing to figure it out if he was willing to do the same.

The kind of love I still felt for Bryson was scary if I was being honest with myself. So there was really no way of just... letting it go. Sure I could've tried to detox myself of everything him, but I really would've just been losing even more of myself in the process.

Just because Bryson had a child on the way didn't mean he was incapable of loving me too.

And he did love me.

In fact, he loved me so much that he was willing to sacrifice his own happiness by really seeing things from my point of view and acknowledging how much sense it made for me to move on.

For a moment, I really believed I was going to do just that. That I was just going to be able to say farewell and move on with my life as if he had never even existed. But then I realized that even in his absence, I was still consumed by him. My thoughts, my feelings, my heart... were out of my hands, out of my control. I had reached the point of no return and I was finally ready to accept it.

I was considering changing my outfit for the

hundredth time when there was a soft knock on the bedroom door. I could pretty much assume it was Landon, so I told him to come on in.

He looked at me through the mirror as he said, "Perfect. You're already dressed. I was gonna see if you wanted to go grab a bite to eat with me."

"Umm... actually, I'm going to dinner with Bryson."

His expression was a mix of confusion and disbelief. "Wait a minute. You're doing, what?"

I rolled my eyes, doing a final touch-up of my makeup as I told him, "Landon, I know you heard me loud and clear, so I'm not gonna repeat it for your listening pleasure."

I could only see his reflection in the mirror, but he appeared completely outdone.

"So you're tellin' me... we were engaged, we both cheated, and you don't even *consider* taking me back. But this dude has a damn baby on the way and he gets to take you to dinner? What kinda shit is that, Kennedy?"

I turned off my lighted vanity mirror before I grabbed my clutch from the bed and went past him out of the bedroom door. Of course he was right on my heels, so I decided to explain, "That's none of your business, Landon. What we had has been over for quite some time now, and while I can understand if this little arrangement had you confused, I'm here to tell you that nothing between us has changed."

I figured that was enough for him to get the point, but clearly I was wrong as he spewed from behind me, "So you'd rather be with the dude who clearly dogged you out and will more than likely rub it in your face for the next however long y'all actually end up being together? You're being a fool, Kennedy."

My hand was already on the doorknob, but that stopped me from turning it.

"Well if I'm such a fool, then why are you still here? Why are *you* so desperate to be with me? Why have you been trying to blind me with your sweet little antics so that I would take *you* back? I'm not the fool here. You're the fool for even thinking for a second that I'd be interested in the likes of you. Now... I'm gonna go, but I suggest your *foolish* ass finds a new place to hang out at cause I'm over this."

He wasted no time challenging, "I'm not going anywhere, Kennedy."

"Well you know what? You don't have to, Landon. *I'll go.* As soon as I get back, I'll pack my things and go." I wasn't sure how any of that was actually going to work, but I'd find a way if that meant I could get away from Landon for good.

Instead of being as mad as I imagined him to be, he actually seemed amused as he said, "Yeah, that's if you aren't too busy crying to me about how Bryson has fucked you over again."

I rolled my eyes so hard I was afraid they'd get stuck. "Your jealousy is *so* not attractive. But true colors will always find a way to show, huh? How about you go find some business of your own, Landon. I'm sure Brandy could use a few more dollars during her set tonight."

Sure, it was a low blow. But quite honestly, I didn't care. And he didn't even have a comeback, just watched me as I walked out of the apartment.

I secretly wished I would never have to come back.

Bryson

I was ready.

Ready to see her, ready to be with her, ready to release all of the feelings I was forced to keep bottled in when we couldn't just... *be.*

I knew it would probably be wise of me to follow her lead so that I didn't overstep, but just thinking about it all had me more anxious than I had ever felt about any one of my "important" basketball games. I knew I looked good, smelled good, and had actually found time to get a haircut. But I still wasn't sure how she'd accept me.

Was she just being friendly or did her new, positive attitude actually mean something?

I prayed for the latter.

I took a peek at my *Rolex* before I looked towards the door of the restaurant I knew she loved since I always caught her having leftovers from the place for lunch. It wasn't exactly the fanciest place I could've found, but I wanted to prove myself as being caring, and observant, and...

Chill, bro.

I peeked up again as she strolled inside looking even better than when I saw her earlier at the parade. She was wearing a simple spaghetti-strap dress that hung onto her lanky frame and flat sandals which I hardly ever saw her wear considering she stayed in heels. Her hair was pulled up into one of those little knot things, putting her high cheekbones on display. And her lips were tinted with red, probably the same color she wore during her interview.

Why do I even remember that?

Because you remember everything about Kennedy.

I smiled as I stood up to wave her over. She looked around for a few seconds before she finally caught my gesture and smiled.

My heart bloomed immediately.

She held her clutch tightly as she squeezed past the other tables to get to me.

And when she did...

I couldn't have pulled her into my arms fast enough.

At first she didn't seem completely sold, but eventually she sighed and fell deeper into my embrace. I pulled away just enough so that I could see her face before I pulled her in once more.

"Bryson, I can't... *breathe.*"

I laughed before I released her just enough again, but not completely. "My bad, Kenn. I just missed you. Like really, *really* missed you." It almost felt a little psychotic how complete I felt just holding her in my arms.

"Well you're really, *really* gonna be missing me when I die from not getting enough air," she teased.

I finally let her go, pulling out a chair for her before finding my own chair. "Hey, don't talk like that."

She waited until I was sitting before she replied with a smile, "I was just joking, Bryson. But how have you been? Living the dream, I'm sure."

She had a light air to her that kind of surprised me, but not enough to deter me from my mission of getting her confidently back on my side.

"To be completely honest with you, right now feels like more of a dream than anything else I've experienced in the last couple weeks."

She looked down to her lap so that I wouldn't see her blushing, but I had caught her anyway. And when she finally did look back up, she tried to change the subject.

"Well how's baby Harris? Do you know what you're having yet?"

Though I hadn't been to an appointment to see for myself yet, I was still proud to share, "A girl."

Her eyes went wide as she immediately started going in. "Ha! Should've known God would give you a girl. They call it punishment for a man when he hasn't treated the women in his life the best. So now you'll get to find out what it's like when a girl comes home crying over a boy who did her dirty."

I shrugged, knowing there may have been some truth to her little statement. But my truth was, "My treatment has never been the issue. It's the honesty they don't seem to like very much." It would take all of my fingers and toes, *plus hers*, to count how many times a woman didn't appreciate my honesty.

Her tone was a little withdrawn as she expressed, "Well I do. Even when it's not good news."

I knew exactly what she was implying. The whole situation was pretty fucked up, but there wasn't much more I could do about it other than beg for her forgiveness.

So that's what I did.

"Kenn baby, I'm so sorry I didn't tell you right away. It was an honest mistake that I own up to completely. I just hope maybe one day you'll forgive me for it."

She took a sip of her wine, then a second before she said, "I've already forgiven you, Bryson. It's the next step I'm afraid of."

Just the mention of a next step had me ready to give her everything I had. But I played it cool and asked, "What do you mean?"

She took a few glances around the restaurant, then another sip of wine, clearly stalling her answer. So I knew I had to assure her, "It's okay, Kennedy. Say what you need to say. I'm all ears."

She sighed, setting her nearly empty glass on the table. "I mean... you're getting ready to be a father, and... I don't know. That's a lot."

"Well according to the notes from Leslie, Nicole has agreed to joint custody. Of course for the first couple of months, the baby will primarily be with her mother. But once she gets a little weight on her, we'll be splitting time."

I could tell Kennedy's mind was running a mile a minute as she lifted her glass to finish it off, then used the back of her hand to swipe her mouth. Her uneasiness about the arrangement made sense, but I had to ask, "Why are you freaking out right now, Kenn?"

She motioned for the waitress to bring her a fresh glass before she answered, "I guess I just... the whole idea of being a wicked stepmother was like the first thing in my head. And considering I'm not even ready to have children of my own, there was no way I was gonna raise someone else's."

A laugh slipped out before I could contain it. The last thing I could ever see Kennedy being was a wicked stepmother. But in the moment, that was beside the fact.

"Kenn, this baby... *my baby*... is nothing for you to worry about. You only have to be as involved as you wanna be, but you don't really *have* to do anything you don't wanna do. *If* you wanna be with me, that is." I couldn't get too ahead of myself, though it felt like things were going in the right direction.

"Bryson, come on now. Do you really think I would've shown up if I didn't wanna be with you? And besides, even if I don't want kids yet that doesn't mean I can't appreciate open-mouthed kisses and unexpected snuggles just as much as the next woman."

My smile grew for more reasons than one. But mainly because, "Kennedy, you'd be pretty sexy with a little baby bump."

She rolled her eyes, taking a quick sip of her newly delivered glass of wine before she said, "Ugh! Don't jinx me like that."

"*What*? I'm just sayin'. Whenever the time comes that a lucky someone gets to plant their seed in that glorious body of yours, it'll be dope. I can already see your little fashionistas strolling around now." I was just sure Kennedy's children would come out of the womb dressed like *Baby Gap* models.

She bit her lip to stifle a grin before she brushed me off. "Oh, whatever. And why'd you say *lucky someone* as if you don't want that person to be you?"

I quickly assured her, "Oh, I most certainly want it to be me. But I'm not ready to press my luck quite yet. Just taking this one thing at a time."

She nodded her head to agree with me, so I continued on. "But I was hoping maybe we could... I don't know. Pick up where we left off?"

I figured I'd attack while she was clearly in a good mood. In all honestly, I would've taken any type of relationship she was willing to give me, even if it was at the basic friendship level.

Would I have pushed the boundaries?

For sure.

But I was willing to restart wherever she saw fit as long as she was going to be in my life in some capacity.

She wore the cutest little smirk as she said, "I'm pretty sure we left off in your bed."

"Perfect. Let's go," I teased, halfway standing up before I sat back down. "Nah, I'm kiddin'. We should probably take our time. Do things the right way."

She didn't seem too enthused about the idea as she

said, "Bryson, if we were really trying to do things the right way, we would've lost the game a long time ago. How about we do things *our* way?"

I nodded to agree with her. "I like the sound of that."

She could only smile, and I was proud knowing I actually had something to do with it. It was the same kind of smile she used to give her phone when ol' boy would hit her up while she was working with me.

Speaking of which...

"Hey, did Landon ever tell you I stopped by before the big game?"

She immediately looked confused as she answered, "What? No!"

Punk ass bitch.

I gave Kennedy the edited version. "That scrub. Is he still hanging around?"

She went back to her withdrawn self, taking another one of those hearty sips of wine before she explained, "Well... we were splitting rent. So since he had paid his part of the rent for the month, he got to stay. And then the stay was extended. Which actually reminds me... I'm kinda homeless right now."

"*Homeless*? Homeless how? Where have you been staying, Kennedy?" I was already ready to beat Landon's ass if he had pulled some weak shit.

She held a hand up as she said, "Relax. I've been at the apartment, but *we*... we got into it, right before I came here actually, and I told him I'd leave."

An idea came to my head instantly.

I tried to hide my excitement as I told her, "Well I have tons of empty rooms for you to choose from if you'd like."

Of course she looked at me like I was crazy. "Bryson, do you really think that's a good idea?"

"Hell yeah. In fact, I think it's a great idea. Best idea

———

I've had all day. So what do you say, roomie?" I was only teasing, knowing the last thing I would ever think of Kennedy as was a roommate.

She looked at me dead-on with a smile as she said, "You're crazy."

"Don't act like you aren't considering it, though. And I won't even charge you rent. It's a win-win situation for the both of us." I couldn't have imagined a better outcome of our little dinner than this one.

If she actually agreed to it.

She eyed me for a long time before she asked, "You're serious, aren't you?"

"Dead serious, Kenn. It gets lonely in that big ol' house by myself. And besides, those few days that you stayed over was the most action some of those rooms have ever seen." The memories of every position we did in every room was still engrained in my head to this day.

She tossed a hand at me, looking partially embarrassed and partially turned on as she said, "Shut up!"

"But seriously, though. I'd be honored if you took me up on the offer. I'll keep my hands to myself and everything."

She challenged me with her eyes over the rim of her wine glass before she said, "That might be the first lie you've ever told me."

We laughed together, and it felt so damn good to not only be in her presence but also be on her good side.

Now I was ready to press my luck.

"So… when do you wanna move your stuff? I mean, unless you'd rather not move that stuff. We can just get you all new stuff." If I had it my way, she wouldn't ever have to step back into her old apartment.

She looked completely amused as she said, "Bryson, you're making this offer a little too good to turn down."

I grinned cheesily as I replied, "Ah, what can I say? I don't really like to hear no if I don't absolutely have to."

She bit her lip as she thought it over and I widened my smile to show her how happy she could be if she said yes; even if the whole thing seemed a little unorthodox, with a hint of crazy, and maybe a hint of...

"Fine."

My heart literally jumped in my chest.

You didn't hear her right, bro.

I swallowed my premature excitement to ask, "Fine?"

She smiled brightly as she nodded her head yes. "Fine. I'll move in with you. *For now*. Until I can find my own place."

I grabbed her hands from across the table, rubbing them with my thumbs as I assured her, "Baby, you know you aren't gonna want to actually leave. In fact, I'm gonna make sure of it. You've already walked out on me enough. I refuse to let it happen again."

Epilogue

Kennedy

So... Bryson was right.

It was exactly a year later, and I still hadn't found my own place, with no intentions of actually doing so. Getting to know Bryson while already living with him was like killing two birds with one stone, though I understood how unique our circumstances were. But I suppose we were just doing things *our* way.

That alone felt amazing.

I made myself busy bouncing Baby Lilah on my thighs like she was in a jumper while she blew spit bubbles in delight. I couldn't believe she was only a few months short of being a one-year-old, her bright eyes and infectious smile giving me baby fever like no other.

Of course, if it was up to her father, we probably would've already gotten started working on a sibling for her. But me bringing a child into the world was completely contingent on one thing - being a wife first.

Baby Lilah was going to have to be plenty for now.

According to the smells coming from her third diaper of the day, she was more than plenty.

"Bryson, Lilah's stinky!" I yelled into the kitchen where he was busy fixing her a bottle.

He strolled into the living room, looking like a total DILF as he tested the bottle's temperature against his wrist before he said, "Well go change her."

I looked to Lilah who was still bouncing in my hands

as I told him, "Nu uh. I did the last one. It's your turn."

He gave me a kiss on the forehead before he tried to give Lilah a couple on her cheek, backing away when he smelled what I had already been hit with.

"Kenn, I gotta call Leslie back. Just do it this one time, then I'll do the next two. Bet?"

I rolled my eyes, standing up with Lilah extended just in case she had had a blow-out.

"I'm gonna hold you to that too, Bryson. So don't even think about dodging it with a phone call from Leslie next time."

He smacked my butt before he laughed and grabbed his phone.

I held Lilah in the air so I could check her clothes before putting her against my waist so we could walk up the stairs. One of Bryson's many guest bedrooms had been transformed into a nursery that was beautifully decorated with soft pink and leopard.

Okay, so maybe I was just tooting my own horn.

I laid Lilah on the changing table before I told her, "I hope you were good to me, little girl. Cause it sure doesn't smell like it."

I reached down to grab a fresh diaper from the stock, then I reached over to grab a wipe. But I realized the box was missing when my hand kept going into its usual space. I looked over and saw that where the box of wipes usually was, there was a small box.

And not just any small box.

"Surprise, baby."

I jumped at the sound of Bryson's voice coming from behind me. My breathing was staggered as I asked, "Bryson... *what is*... what is this?"

"What does it look like, Kennedy?" he teased, making me smack him on the chest, already on the verge of tears.

244

He picked up the box, then he dropped down to one knee in front of me. My hands flew to my face in disbelief as he cracked the box open, revealing the most beautiful diamond I had ever seen.

Now the tears were real.

"Kenn baby, you stole a piece of me the second you strolled into that interview. You've been nothing but a blessing over this past year we've spent together, and hell, even before that. So will you *please* do me the honor of being Mrs. Harris?"

I couldn't answer with real words, so instead I frantically shook my head yes. He slid the ring on my finger with a giddy smile before he stood up, wiped my tears, and pulled me into a hug so tight it lifted me off of my feet. Even Baby Lilah looked happy as she rocked side-to-side on the changing table with a smile like she had any idea of what was going on.

Bryson put me down eventually but didn't let me go as he peppered soft kisses all over my face.

Even in the bliss of the moment, I couldn't help teasing, "So I guess bomb ass pussy really *does* get a proposal before the two-year mark, huh?"

He gave me a lingering kiss on the forehead as he confessed, "Baby, I was ready to propose to you the first night I tasted it in the strip club."

I slapped him on the chest again; this time a little harder to do with the rock he had put on my finger.

"Oh my God! I can't stand you, Bryson."

He only smiled proudly, holding me tight as he said, "I love you too, Mrs. Harris. I love... you... *too*."

The End

Enjoyed this book?
Please leave a review on
Amazon or Goodreads!

To stay up-to-date with all
of Alexandra Warren's
happenings including samples
and excerpts, visit
actuallyitsalexandra.com or
like her **Facebook** page!

More Books by Alexandra
Warren
**Attractions & Distractions
Series
Getting The Edge
An Unconventional Love
The PreGame Ritual**

Check out a sample from,
The PreGame Ritual, featuring
Bryson's little brother Miles!

Ava knows that she's the best girls basketball player in the country at the collegiate level.

She knows that she's going straight the pros once her senior season comes to an end.

And she knows that finding a man is the least likely thing to happen while she's chasing that dream.

That's until she meets Miles.
A freshman phenom who has no idea what college life is like but is in for a red-headed surprise with a mean crossover.

Their chemistry is a given, but will age be more than just a number?
Or will the PreGame Ritual be enough to even the score?

ava.

How many times must a girl watch *Love & Basketball* before she realizes that shit is just a movie?

I mean, I've had my share of pick-up basketball games against the boys.

I've had my share of athlete boyfriends.

And I've had my share of breakups to makeups.

Yet, there was no inkling of a *Quincy* involved.

Being in my senior year at Lynstone University, it was a known fact that I would graduate and play professional ball; first in the states, then most likely overseas since that was where the real money in women's basketball was made. But it was also beginning to *feel* like a known fact that I would be doing it all as a single woman.

It wasn't like I was even looking for a relationship. But in the same, I wouldn't mind if it somehow, some way found me.

Between school and basketball, I was kept pretty busy, so I really didn't have much time for the boys anyway. But when I did have time, I surely didn't want to spend every minute of it watching *Love & Basketball* alone in my apartment.

Of course, while I spent my Friday night with popcorn and my favorite movie, my roommate/little sister Avery was spending it out on the town with some dude she had probably just met during the week. Avery was completely opposite of me. She didn't play sports, she loved getting all dolled up in dresses and heels even for a regular ass Tuesday, and she bounced between boyfriends more than I bounced my basketballs.

I couldn't knock her game, though. Cause truth be told, I wished I was out too.

The movie came to an end and I wiped my tears before I changed the channel to *ESPN*. They were giving a rundown of the players to watch from each college and I noticed my school was next up on the list. I figured they were going to talk about Darrell Sims, *one of my best guy friends*, since he was considered the star of the team and was team captain. But to my surprise, they brought up a little freshman they described as a, "Phenom". They bragged on and on about how good he was in high school and how he had the potential to take a starter's spot. They cut to an interview with the little dude, and even more surprisingly, he wasn't little at all.

He was... *a freshman*.

A cute ass, kinda grown ass looking freshman.

Hmph, must've been held back a few times.

I knew most of the guys on the team because we shared practice facilities, so I wasn't sure how I had missed this... *kid*. My eyes were glued to the screen as they asked him about what he thought of the team so far, how he was enjoying college, and if he was going to try to go pro after his freshman year. He gave a little laugh, flashing a smile that embarrassingly went straight to my southern half.

Damn girl, you need some action.

I don't know why I was even wasting my time sweatin' him through the television as if it was possible to give somebody so young the time of day. I mean, surely he was still caught up on chasing fast ass girls and building his playa resume. He wouldn't even know what to do with a woman like me. A woman with goals, and dreams, and visions, and an actual life compared to the

—

young broads who were busy trying to chase after him instead of chase after something of their own.

The screen cut to the next college, and I let my thoughts of him cut right with it.

miles.

College was the shit.

I only had to be in class for a few hours out of the day, then spend a few hours at the court or in the weight room, and the rest of the day was mine. I had a feeling things would change once the season started. But for now, college was feeling a little like heaven.

I was just finishing up a workout session with the team when I saw the girls' basketball players heading our way. We crossed paths on occasion, but I hardly ever paid them any mind cause, *keeping it real*, a few of them looked manlier than me. I gave a, *"What's-up"* nod to the few I was familiar with before I grabbed my towel to clean off the sweat I had worked up.

Since I was dead tired, I decided to find a seat in the bleachers next to some of my teammates who were still hanging around. We watched the girls do their warm-ups which were pretty similar to ours - a light jog, a few lay-up drills, and a few passing drills. One of the girls threw a bad pass, and the ball flew into the bleachers right over my head.

"Yo Miles, you better watch out up there," yelled my boy, Cam, before he gave a laugh. I shrugged him off and reached behind me to grab the ball, planning to pass it back to the court. Instead, I turned around right into a pair of titties that were squeezing against one of the familiar practice jerseys.

When I looked up from her chest, I found a pair of scolding eyes and flat-lined lips. "Damn, you act like you've never seen boobs before. Give me the ball, bro."

I handed it to her before she strided back down the bleachers and onto the court. Once she was out of earshot, my teammates couldn't wait to clown me.

"Bruhhh, are you a virgin or somethin'? I swear you were on stuck for a minute straight lookin' at her rack."

"Nah, man. I was just... reading her jersey." That was easily the worst lie I could've came up with considering their practice jerseys were identical to ours.

"Bullshit. Everybody knows Ava has some big ass titties. I bet she has to wear two or three sports bras a game."

All the boys laughed, but my eyes were back on the girl I now knew was named Ava. She was gorgeous, with her long, red hair pulled back into a high ponytail accessorized with a *Nike* headband and a face so flawless you would've thought she was in one of those face wash commercials. I was sure a lot of her shape was muted by the baggy practice gear, but there were still undeniable hints of an athletic but womanly frame. She looked *nothing* like the other girls I knew on the team.

How the hell did I miss her?

I watched intently as she dribbled down the court, giving a little crossover before she set up the play for her team. She quickly realized how scrambled the defense was and dribbled right past her defender at the speed of light into an easy lay-up. It was a textbook move, but she did it with a finesse that only an experienced baller could do it.

"Ava is the fuckin' truth, man. I don't know why she keeps actin' like she doesn't wanna talk to ya boy."

I didn't want to sound too thirsty for the details, but I couldn't help asking, "You tried to talk to her before?"

"Hell yeah. A couple times. But ever since I messed with her little sister, she's not feelin' me."

—

Well, duh.

Instead of responding to Cam, I focused my attention back on Ava. She was hanging out at the three-point line with her hands on her knees and her ponytail slung against her shoulder while one of her teammates shot a pair of free throws. Even though the girl missed the first free throw, Ava still went in and gave her a pat on the back before pointing out to her teammates what defense they were going to go into once the girl shot the second free throw. Every one of her teammates listened attentively, and it was then that I knew just how in control she was.

It was sexy as hell.

"Miles, pick up your lip, dude. You don't stand a chance with Ava."

"Who said I wanted a chance with Ava?"

Even though in my head I knew it was the truth, it was the last thing I wanted somebody like Cam to know. We were cool and all, but it didn't take long for me to recognize that he was a talker. Meaning if he had any idea what I was even *thinking*, it would be campus news before I could make it home that night.

"That drool hangin' from your lip said it all."

I gave my lips a quick swipe and found out Cam was just fuckin' with me. He laughed me off as he said, "Gullible ass. You got a lot to learn, freshman."

NOW AVAILABLE

Made in the USA
Middletown, DE
22 September 2021